UNEXPECTED VISITOR!

Frank and Joe wriggled hard and fast over the last twenty yards of the tunnel. Joe finally pulled himself out of the hole and into a cavern.

The cavern looked like a smaller version of the one they'd just spent almost an hour crawling from. The roof was lower, but the rock formations were equally spectacular.

Standing in front of the mouth of the tunnel, Joe could feel the cave breeze, with its strange, mossy smell. For a second he thought he heard a light rattling sound, like a wind chime made out of hollow wooden tubes. He sensed a spindly shadow out of the corner of his eye and turned toward it. When his head lamp fell full on it, Joe let out a gasp.

The hand of a human skeleton was dangling inches from his face.

Books in THE HARDY BOYS CASEFILES™ Series

THE HARDY BOYS

CASEFILES™

NO. 115

CAVE TRAP

FRANKLIN W. DIXON

AN ARCHWAY PAPERBACK
Published by POCKET BOOKS
New York London Toronto Sydney Tokyo Singapore

This book is a work of fiction. Names, characters, places and incidents are products of the author's imagination or are used fictitiously. Any resemblance to actual events or locales or persons, living or dead, is entirely coincidental.

AN ARCHWAY PAPERBACK *Original*

An Archway Paperback published by
POCKET BOOKS, a division of Simon & Schuster Inc.
1230 Avenue of the Americas, New York, NY 10020

Copyright © 1996 by Simon & Schuster Inc.
Produced by Mega-Books, Inc.

ISBN: 0-671-50462-2

First Archway Paperback printing September 1996

10 9 8 7 6 5 4 3 2 1

THE HARDY BOYS, AN ARCHWAY PAPERBACK and colophon are registered trademarks of Simon & Schuster Inc.

THE HARDY BOYS CASEFILES is a trademark of Simon & Schuster Inc.

Cover photograph from "The Hardy Boys" Series © 1995 Nelvana Limited/Marathon Productions S.A. All rights reserved.

Logo design TM & © 1995 by Nelvana Limited. All rights reserved.

Printed in the U.S.A.

IL 6+

Chapter

1

THE BUS CAME BARRELING around a curve and screeched to a halt.

"Whoa!" Joe Hardy shouted, bracing himself against the seat in front of him.

"Everybody okay back there?" the driver asked. They had been climbing a steep, curved road just outside a small hamlet in the Kentucky hill country. There wasn't a traffic light or another village within miles. Joe and his older brother, Frank, were the only passengers on the bus.

"We're fine," Frank said, craning his neck to see out the front window. "What happened?"

"It's a road block, fellas," the driver said. "Some kind of protest. We'll just have to wait till they clear it."

"Oh, man," Joe said, glancing at his watch impatiently. "We're never going to make it to Dismal Hollow in time to meet Dr. Beasley."

"They're completely blocking the road," Frank said.

Joe got up, crouching so he wouldn't bump his head on the luggage rack. Out the front window he could see about twenty protesters sitting cross-legged in the middle of the road with their arms linked. They were chanting, "Hey ho! Hey ho! Kentucky Coal has got to go!" Two state police cruisers and a van were parked on the shoulder of the road, lights flashing.

"It's going to take the cops at least a half hour to clear those people off the road," Joe said. Two state troopers were picking the protesters off the pavement one at a time and carrying them to the back of the van.

"By the time we get to the hollow, Beasley's going to be long gone," Joe continued. "We should have rented a car at the airport."

"And then what?" Frank said. "Run those people over? I checked the map. This is the only route up to Dismal Hollow."

Lining the road were about fifty more activists who were shouting and chanting and holding signs that read Marvin West—Martyred for Mother Earth and Marvin West—Killed for Coal. Several of them wore T-shirts with the slogan Nature First—People for a Sane Envi-

ronmental Policy and a picture of the earth surrounded by a cloud of black smoke.

With traffic at a standstill, some of the heck-
lers from the roadside started banging on the
sides of the bus. One of them looked up at Joe
and yelled, "You got any coal moles on that
bus? We're going to dig them out if you do."

Frank sat back in his seat and said, "They're
really ticked off, aren't they?"

"I guess I'd be ticked off, too," Joe said, plop-
ping back down in his seat. "First, they find out
the coal company might be tunneling under the
state park. They protest with sit-ins at the headquarters and the mine entrances, and then one
of their guys winds up on the wrong end of a
hit-and-run accident. There's got to be a con-
nection."

"Maybe so," Frank said, "but don't forget,
we stay out of whatever is happening between
Nature First and the coal company. We focus
on the expedition—and that's it."

Frank was right, Joe thought, as he recalled
their father's briefing the night before. Fenton
Hardy had been very clear on what their role
would be in the case. They were on a secret
assignment for the Environmental Protection
Agency, the federal agency in charge of enforc-
ing environmental laws.

"You're going under cover *and* underground," he'd said. "I got you assigned to a caving expedition led by the prominent geologist Dr. Nicholas Beasley. The goal of the expedition is to find a link between Cathedral Cave and an isolated cave system in the Dismal Hollow region."

"You mean *the* Cathedral Cave?" Joe had said. "The one with the underground lake?"

"That's the one."

"Sounds great, Dad," Frank had answered. "So what's our goal and the goal of the EPA?"

"You'll be posing as representatives of the Bayport chapter of the National Young Geologists Club. You'll be assisting Dr. Beasley. If he finds a link between the two caving systems, it'll be a major find.

"I was hired to check out Beasley's possible connections to Kentucky Coal and Shale. The folks at the EPA think the company may have hired somebody to infiltrate the expedition or bribed one of the expedition members to prospect for coal along the way."

"Why would they make such a big secret about prospecting for coal?" Frank had wondered.

"Because it's illegal," Fenton had replied. "Recently, Kentucky Coal and Shale bought up thousands of acres of land along the northern border of Cathedral Cave State Park. They've been doing some prospecting up there, all of it legitimate, but they haven't found much coal. Rumor has it that they're drilling under park borders now and they may have found something. The park's been in touch with the EPA and the FBI about possible boundary violations.

"Dr. Beasley's expedition is starting from a sixty-acre parcel near the state park. It's practically the only private land left in the area."

"So Beasley's the one to watch?" Joe had asked.

"Not necessarily," Fenton had replied. "There's a party of six or seven, and the Kentucky Coal spy could be any of them. That's assuming there is a spy. Let's see, there are a couple of scientists, a park ranger, and I understand the owner of the property, a Mr. McCall, will also be going along. We just need to figure out who's who and whether anything illegal is going on."

It took the troopers about twenty-five minutes to clear all the protestors from the road. Then they waved the bus on. Within half an hour, it pulled over to the side of the deserted two-lane highway. The front door opened with a hiss of air from its hydraulics, and the driver announced, "Dismal Hollow. Step lively."

Frank and Joe moved to the front of the bus. "Are you sure this is it?" Joe asked the driver. "It looks like the middle of nowhere."

"Son, I've been driving this route for twenty-three years, and I'm as sure as the cock crows at dawn." The driver stepped down from his seat. "I'll get your luggage for you."

Frank peered at the empty road in front of the bus. The woods were thick on both sides, shading the asphalt from the brutal August sun. Rising above the treetops to the right of the road was a steep cliff, its craggy face bearded with green brush and overhanging saplings.

"Not a house in sight," Frank said over his shoulder to Joe. "And no welcoming party either."

"We're almost an hour late," Joe said. "Maybe they went to call the bus company to figure out why."

"Could be," Frank said, following the bus driver out the door and onto the gravel at the side of the road. After being used to the air-conditioning on the bus, the boys were hit by the oppressive heat of a late-summer Kentucky afternoon. The bus driver pulled two eighty-pound knapsacks on aluminum frames, each with a bedroll strapped to the hip belt, out of the luggage compartment.

Frank arched his back and stretched his six-foot-one-inch frame. After two hours on a plane from New York to Louisville, Kentucky, then another two hours on a bus to Dismal Hollow, he was feeling pretty stiff.

Joe stretched, too, then pulled a plastic canteen out of the side-pocket of his pack. "I'm glad I filled this up back at the airport," he said, after a few big gulps.

"Don't chug it all," Frank said. "We may need it later. Who knows how long we're going to have to wait."

After the bus pulled off, they glanced up and down the empty road. The woods were thick with late-summer foliage. The only sound was the constant droning of cicadas in the background.

"I guess we'll just have to wait till rush hour and hitch a ride," Joe said.

"How about we take a look at your map," Frank said, "instead of standing around and making lame jokes."

"How about we read that sign over there, instead of looking at my map?" Joe said. He pointed to a weather-beaten board nailed to a tree at the edge of the woods. A boysenberry bush had grown up in front of it, partly blocking it from view. Frank went over and pushed aside the leaves to reveal a faded handpainted message: Cave Tours by Local Expert. $3. Ask for Pop McCall.

"McCall," Frank said. "That's the name of the property owner who's going along on the expedition." He peered into the woods, checking out the narrow dirt track leading up the mountain in the direction of the ridge.

Judging from the condition of the sign and how overgrown the bushes were, Frank guessed it had been a long time since any tourist had gone up that road and taken a tour.

"I guess we ought to head up that way," Joe said, moving toward the dirt road. "I hope it isn't too far."

"I think we're better off waiting," Frank said. "If they come back and we're not here, they might think we never showed up."

Joe must not have heard Frank because he just kept on going.

"Hold it," Frank said, hurrying to catch up with Joe.

"Look, we're going to get there one way or another," Joe said. "The sooner the better. Besides, I don't want to end up like Marvin West."

"What are you talking about?" Frank said.

"Wake up, Frank," Joe said. "He's the guy they found on a back road up in the mountains."

"I know that," Frank said.

"He was run over three times," Joe continued. "Dad showed me the pictures. There were skid marks on the asphalt. The driver hit him, backed over him, then ran over him again just to make sure he was dead."

"So?" Frank said. "Just because one guy gets

creamed on a lonely highway doesn't mean we're—"

Before he could finish his sentence, the sharp crack of a gunshot ripped through the still summer air. Frank spun around and dropped to the ground in a heap.

Chapter

2

As FRANK HIT THE DIRT, Joe heard another shot and then a shout of "Yee-haw!" echoing through the woods. Frank was sprawled in the road about four feet away.

"Frank, are you all right?" Joe said.

Frank tested his arms and legs gingerly and then raised his head. "I think so. What happened?"

"Well, unless the back of your head is missing," Joe said, "I think the bullet went through your pack."

Frank reached back and felt two ragged holes on either side of his pack. "Feels like my shaving cream is leaking," he said.

They heard someone crashing through the

bushes and charging toward them. Joe slipped out of the shoulder straps of his backpack and rolled into a fern-covered ditch beside the road.

Frank didn't have time to duck out of sight so he lay still, playing dead. A brawny, bearded man carrying a rifle burst through the foliage about ten feet away.

"I know I got me one," the man said. "Now, where'd the other one go?"

Joe held his breath, listening to the crunch of the man's boots on the ground. A second later the fern fronds rustled and Joe looked up to see the business end of the rifle poking through the foliage just inches from his temple. The bearded gunman was squinting down the sights right at Joe's head.

"Git outta that gully, boy," he said.

"Careful with that gun," Joe said, emerging from the ferns with his hands raised high. "I'm not armed." The man's beard was as thick as a raccoon pelt, and his bushy eyebrows shaded a pair of deep-set eyes that fixed Joe with a predator's glare. He was wearing a pair of bib overalls that were a couple of sizes too big and streaked with mud. The brim of a battered hat shaded his forehead.

"How many times I got to tell you folks, this here land's private," bellowed the rugged mountain man. "I'm sick of your dang-fooled snoopin' around my daddy's property. I done warned you yesterday I'd kill the next one that shows his face in these parts, and now I aim to make good on my promise." He cocked his rifle.

Frank dived at the back of the gunman's knees and the gun went off. The shot went wild, high into the treetops. Then Joe leapt on him, knocking the rifle aside and pinning his shoulders to the dirt. The big man tried to kick free, but Frank had his legs in a solid grasp.

Joe kneeled on the man's chest and held down his wrists. Breathing hard, Joe glared into the man's face and spat out, "You've got a trigger finger that's way too itchy for my taste, pal."

Even with one hundred eighty pounds of Hardy muscle pinning him to the ground, the man was defiant. "You had your warning yesterday," he growled. "I told you I'd shoot you."

"We weren't here yesterday," Joe said through gritted teeth. "We just got here. Next time, why don't you ask before you start blasting?"

"All right, all right," the man said. "Whyn't you let me up and we'll work this out peacefully? I'm sorry if I scared you boys, but this is private property."

"Okay," Joe said. "But if you try anything, my brother and I are going to break your thick skull."

Joe let go of the man's wrists, got up, and scooped up the rifle in one smooth motion. The bearded man rose slowly, watching Joe carefully as he wiped his hands on his overalls. Then, a smile broke out on his lips, and he started to chuckle. "You mean to tell me you ain't—" Laughter bubbled out of his massive chest.

Joe glanced at Frank, who was frowning. "What's so funny?" Joe demanded. "You almost killed my brother."

Before the man could reply, they all heard the sound of a vehicle approaching. Joe turned to see a four-by-four pickup truck pull around the bend. When he turned back, he saw his prisoner taking off down the slope, leaping over bushes and between trees.

"Hey!" Joe shouted. He started to go after him, but Frank caught his arm and said, "Let him go. He can't do anything without that rifle."

The truck pulled up to a stop. It had a Cathedral Cave State Park Rangers insignia on its door. A woman dressed in a crisp khaki uniform and a ranger's hat leaned out the window and said, "Were you the ones shooting just now?"

"No, ma'am," Joe said. "It was that guy, he just took off down the—"

"Are you Frank and Joe Hardy from Bayport?" she asked. "I was sent to pick you up."

Frank stuck out his hand, and the woman looked at it without shaking it. "So, you've signed up for Dr. Beasley's expedition?"

"Yep," Joe said.

"You're late," she said. "I waited for your bus for half an hour. I couldn't wait any longer. I had an appointment."

"Sorry," Frank said. "The bus got delayed by the protesters."

"I'm Debbie Cameron, and I'm part of the expedition, too. I'm representing the interests of Cathedral Cave State Park." She looked disapprovingly at the rifle Joe held, saying, "I'm afraid firearms aren't allowed on underground expeditions."

"It's not ours," Frank explained. "We just got shot at by a guy who came crashing out of the woods."

"Oh, really?" she said. "And then he turned around and gave you his gun?"

"No," Joe replied. "We—"

"That's all right, just get in," she said, releasing the emergency brake and gunning the motor. "You can save the rest of your story till we get up to camp."

They hoisted their packs into the bed of the pickup truck, then hopped in and sat on a stack of new rope, which was carefully coiled and labeled. They braced themselves as the truck pulled a quick U-turn and went bouncing up the steep, rocky road. After about twenty minutes, a cabin came into sight through the trees. Frank guessed they were near the top of the ridge they'd seen from the road.

The cabin clung to a steep embankment. It had a wide porch that jutted out over the driveway, forming a partial roof for an old, broken-down truck, whose axles rested on cinder blocks where tires had once been. Several of the cabin's weathered clapboards hung at odd angles, and there were scabs of flaking paint everywhere.

A hundred yards below the cabin there was a brand-new van with the words University of Kentucky—Geology Department stenciled on the door. A massive pile of tangled rope lay in the middle of the road.

A smallish young man in his twenties, wearing a red tank top, stood next to an aluminum folding table, speaking to two younger men. He was holding a clipboard and pointing to an impressive collection of cam-loaded clips, webbed load-bearing belts, fasteners, gloves, and other caving equipment arranged neatly on the table.

He introduced himself as Spencer Lugo. "I'm Dr. Beasley's assistant," he said. "I'm a graduate student in the geology department at the University of Kentucky." Gesturing to the two younger men, Lugo said, "And this is Pat and Alex Gallagher. They're undergrads at Kentucky. They'll be the surface-level support team, ferrying equipment between the campsite and our base camp underground."

"Nice to meet you," Frank said. The Gallagher brothers were obviously twins. Both had wiry, close-cut black hair and fair skin. They looked about nineteen.

Glancing at his clipboard, Spencer said, "I'm glad you guys finally made it. We could use some help carrying this equipment to the mouth of the cave. It's about a two-mile trek down into the hollow."

Debbie Cameron reached into the back of her truck, lifted out the rifle, and unloaded it.

"You guys aren't expecting to bring that along, are you?" Spencer said.

"It's not ours," Frank said. "Since the bus was so late, we decided to hike up. Then this wild man started taking potshots at my head." He glanced at Debbie. "The sound of your truck must have scared him off. He sort of left his rifle behind."

"Sounds like Buddy," Spencer said.

"Yep," Debbie said, with a slight smile and a shake of her head. "This looks like his gun."

"Who's Buddy?" Frank said.

"He's the one-man Dismal Hollow welcoming committee," she said. "And you just got the red-carpet treatment."

"Unfortunately, we've been having some problems around here," Spencer said. "Conflicts between the Nature First people, some bankers, and certain local residents." He glanced up at the cabin on the hillside above them. "Pop McCall—he's the owner of this land—assured the safety of our expedition. Which means his son, Buddy, is policing the property. That's their cabin up there. Pop likes to sit out on the porch."

Frank took a closer look at the porch, which hung out over the rusty truck. From that angle, Frank couldn't see much, but finally made out a man's face peering between the slats of the porch railing. Frank stared and the man steadily returned his gaze.

Just then Dr. Beasley emerged from the van. "Did you get the rope?" he asked Debbie.

"Just like you told me," she replied, reaching into the back of her truck. "I had to go all the way to Cave City, and it wasn't cheap."

"That comes out of your pay, Spencer," Dr. Beasley said.

"That's not fair," Spencer said. "I told you, it was an accident."

"What happened?" Joe said.

"Who are you?" Beasley asked, noticing Frank and Joe for the first time.

"We're Frank and Joe Hardy," Joe said. "The assistants you hired from the Bayport NYGC. Sorry we're late. Our bus got held up by a Nature First protest."

"Ah, yes. Well, then, welcome aboard," Beasley said. "We could use the extra help to get this expedition going."

"About that rope," Frank said.

"There's been some disagreement about that," Dr. Beasley said. "But one thing's for sure. The rope we brought from the university is useless. Somebody splattered battery acid on it." He looked at Spencer.

"I told you before, I don't know how it got there," Spencer said. "I'm only supposed to be—"

"Skip it," Beasley interrupted. "The point is, we're lucky I noticed it. You can barely see where the acid ate into the rope." He glanced over at the pile of tangled rope. "If I hadn't gone over it one last time, we might not have known about it until it broke."

Joe knelt to inspect the pile in the driveway. It looked brand-new. It was three-quarter-inch nylon rope, mostly shiny and white, with a braided thread of blue running like a dotted line along its length. Joe ran the rope through his fingers until he felt a slight imperfection. A closer look revealed a slight stain where the battery acid had dried.

"This looks good," Beasley said, checking the new rope Debbie had bought, "but it'll have to be washed." He glanced up at Debbie.

"Whoa, Nick," she said. "I don't mind running an errand or two or hauling equipment to the campsite at the mouth of the cave, but—"

"I'll do it," Frank said quickly. He figured it

was a chance to make himself useful and at the same time have a talk with old Mr. McCall.

"Good," Dr. Beasley said. He handed Frank a scrub pad and a bucket. "Dishwashing soap should do fine. You just want to get rid of any lubricants left over from the factory. And make sure the sheath tightens around the core. Meanwhile, we'll start ferrying this equipment to the campsite."

With the rope coiled around his shoulder, Frank started to climb up the steep slope to the porch. Debbie stopped him and handed him the rifle. "This ought to be returned to its owner," she said.

When Frank reached the porch, he found an old man sitting in a split-cane rocking chair, wrapped in blankets. "Mr. McCall?" Frank said. "I think this belongs to your son." He rested the firearm next to the screen door.

The old man was bald, shrunken, and wrinkled. He gazed at Frank from under a grizzled brow for a long moment, then said, "How'd you git it?"

"My brother and I took it from him," Frank said, "after he shot at us."

McCall nodded. His expression didn't change. "I'll make sure to tell him when he gits back," he said finally.

"Can I get some soap and water to wash this rope?" Frank said.

"Bucket's out back by the pump," the old man said. "Soap's in the kitchen, long as Beasley can replace it."

Frank found a rusty hand pump at the top of a hand-dug well behind the cabin. He brought the bucket of soapy water back to the porch and started running the rope through it.

"Most folks wouldn't know that a new rope needs washin' before it's used," Pop McCall said. "I guess yer boss knows what he's doin'."

"I guess he does," Frank said. "But I'd be willing to bet you know more."

The old man chuckled, but the chuckle soon turned into a dry, rattling cough. "I guess I do know something," he said. "I been looking for a link to Cathedral Cave my whole life. But that's all over."

"What do you mean?" Frank said. "Aren't you going with us?"

McCall shook his head. "I wish I could, but I had me a bad spell with my heart, and Doc says I can't go underground no more."

"That's too bad," Frank said.

"I know that link is there," the old man said. "I can smell it when I'm down there. You might, too. It's like pond water, mixed with a sort of spicy smell. You can't mistake it."

"If we find it," Frank said, "it'll really put Dismal Hollow on the map."

"Don't I know it," McCall said. "I'd be rich

20

and famous, and them bank officers wouldn't dare foreclose on my property."

"Foreclose?" Frank repeated. "You mean—"

"Nah, we made the payment this month," McCall said. "Thanks to the contract Dr. Beasley signed with me."

"Contract?" Frank said.

"Yup," McCall said. "I got it inside. It spells out all the rules and regulations of the expedition."

Frank finished washing the rope and hung the coiled loops over the porch railing to dry. "I'll just dump this water out back," he said.

McCall nodded. As Frank stepped down onto the top step of the porch, a hand suddenly gripped his ankle and yanked his foot out from under him. The bucket of soapy water went flying, and Frank slid sideways down the steps.

Chapter

3

FRANK CAUGHT A GLIMPSE of Buddy McCall scrambling out from under the porch. He tried to roll away, but Buddy dived and landed on him like a linebacker.

Frank tried to break free as the two rolled down the steep slope toward the driveway. Buddy was too strong, though, and he pinned Frank on his back with a huge forearm pressed across his windpipe.

"That'll teach ya to clip me from behind like you did back in the woods," Buddy grumbled.

"Buddy," Mr. McCall yelled from the porch. "Git yer hands off the boy. He's with the expedition."

"Okay, Pop," Buddy said, loosening his grip.

Frank scrambled to his feet and started dusting off his clothes. "Sorry, Buddy," he said, "but you were about to shoot my brother. I had to take you down."

"I wouldn't have shot him," Buddy said. "Just like I didn't shoot you. You know I was just trying to scare you boys. We've had some of them bank officials snoopin' around my daddy's land out here. Tellin' us we gotta get out. Sometimes the only thing folks will listen to is a rifle."

"We tried to tell you who we were," Frank said, "but you didn't stick around long enough to find out."

Buddy grinned. "I know when I've been licked, boy. That's why I took off. Now I just wanted to git even." He extended his brawny hand to Frank. "I'm Buddy," he said. "No hard feelings, I hope."

Pop McCall's quavering voice came from the porch above their heads. "Buddy, git on up here. I been out in the sun too long."

"Would you help me put him inside?" Buddy said to Frank. "He's been sick."

Frank helped Buddy carry Mr. McCall into the house. If he was too weak to walk into his own house, he sure wasn't strong enough to go on any caving expedition, Frank thought. While Buddy was attending to his father in the bedroom, Frank stayed in the living room. With all the shades drawn, it was dim, but Frank could

23

make out some legal documents on the table
next to the couch.

Glancing over his shoulder to make sure he
was alone, Frank sat on the couch and looked
at the papers. The first was a standard rental
contract, stipulating how much the expedition
would pay Pop McCall. It was signed by both
Beasley and Pop. The second document was
more interesting. It was a restrictive covenant
that limited the use of the McCall land for all
time no matter who owned it. It ruled out any
mining, drilling, testing, or extracting of minerals from under the property. Frank saw there
was a place for Pop McCall's signature, but it
hadn't been signed yet.

Frank heard Buddy's footsteps, and he managed to slip the papers back onto the table before Buddy saw what he was doing.

"Doc says Pop's got a bad ticker," Buddy
said. "If we had us some money, they could do
some surgery down at the regional medical
center."

"I wish I could help," Frank said.

Buddy looked him in the eye. "If y'all find
that link to Cathedral Cave, that'll do the trick.
They'll start busing the tourists in, and we'll
charge admission. Pop can get his surgery, and
we can fix this place up some."

"And if there's no link?" Frank said.

"Well, then, Pop's done for, and I guess the bank or somebody else will get this land."

"Like maybe the coal company?" Frank said.

"That depends," Buddy said. "If y'all find a big fat vein of one hundred percent pure anthracite instead, it might just bail us out, too."

"I should get this rope down to the camp," Frank said.

"It's right down that trail over yonder," Buddy said as they walked out onto the porch. "I'll be down later to pay a visit."

"See you later, Buddy."

The trail over the ridge and down into the hollow was easy to follow. After about half an hour, Frank came to the crest of the ridge. Looking down through the thick foliage, he could see why they called it a hollow. Steep slopes plunged down into a narrow gorge, where there was a creek tumbling over stones far below. Mist rose from the creek bed and hung in the listless air.

Frank heard a splash from down below, then a whoop of delight. He hustled down the steep trail, steadying himself on roots and branches as he went. Within ten minutes, he reached the bank of the creek at the bottom of the hollow, where he found the Gallagher twins in the shallow water, cooling off.

Joe, Debbie Cameron, and Spencer Lugo stood on the bank of the creek, but they weren't watching the twins. They were looking up at a cliff overhanging the stream. Frank followed their gaze and saw Dr. Beasley, grasping onto branches and toe holds on the face of the cliff, pulling himself onto a ledge about twenty feet up. Once he stepped onto the ledge, he turned, waved, then disappeared from sight.

"Is that the cave mouth?" Frank asked Debbie.

Debbie nodded. "You can't see much from down here with all those vines hanging over it."

Dr. Beasley's head reappeared over the ledge. "It looks good," he said. "Spencer, I want you to take some shock imager readings, pronto."

"Okay," Spencer called back up. He turned to Joe. "Want to help out?"

"Sure," Joe said.

Dr. Beasley called down, "Frank, why don't you hang that rope up to dry now? Then we'll head back up to the truck to pick up another load of gear."

Beasley climbed down from the cave mouth, and he was clearly excited. "It looks very promising, better than I expected."

"As I said," Spencer said, "I saw a lot of caves, and this one definitely looked like the deepest."

"We'll set up base camp tomorrow," Beasley said, "and then start exploring. Let's head back up for another load."

26

Frank went over to drape the rope on some trees and bushes to dry. Joe followed him.

"It sure is hot," Frank said. "Guess you lucked out, Joe."

Joe grinned. "They tell me these caves keep a consistent temperature of fifty-five degrees— sounds like air conditioning to me."

"Joe," Frank said, lowering his voice. "When I was inside the cabin helping Buddy with the old man I sneaked a peek at some papers in there." He explained the two contracts he'd seen.

"If anyone from the coal company finds out about that restrictive covenant," Joe said, "they're going to do whatever they can to try to stop Pop from signing it. Do you think we should tell Buddy?"

"No, I don't want to risk blowing our cover so soon," Frank said. "But I might be able to find out what Debbie knows about it."

"Meanwhile, I'll see what Lugo's story is," Joe said.

"See you later," Frank said, hustling back up the trail toward the cabin.

Joe went over to join Spencer, who was starting to unpack their gear.

"Have you ever used one of these?" Lugo asked, showing Joe the carbide lamp on his helmet.

Joe shook his head. Spencer took a chunk of

27

carbide, which looked like graphite—plain pencil lead—out of a sealed box. "Carbide is basically safe to use if you handle it carefully. You have to keep the carbide in a waterproof container because it reacts to moisture by fizzing and releasing acetylene gas. Then you just put it in your lamp and light it. As long as you keep the jets clean, it's the best underground light available."

"Sure looks a lot easier than carrying batteries and flashlights," Joe said.

Spencer nodded. "There is a pollution risk, though," he said. "You have to carry out the spent carbon. You can't just dump it in the cave. In fact, they banned carbide lamps from Cathedral Cave because of all the soot people used to dump."

He showed Joe how to load the carbide into the chamber behind the light. A small vial of water locked into a second chamber. With a twist of a lever the mechanism started to hiss. When Spencer held a match to the jet, the lamp sputtered a couple of times, then glowed brightly. "That's why you should always carry plenty of waterproof matches when you're in the cave," Spencer said. "Without your light, you're blind. And you can't start these babies without a match."

"What's this stuff on the inside of the helmet?" Joe asked.

"That's an emergency thermal blanket," Spencer said. "You'll probably never have to use it, but keep it in there. You never know. And it makes a nice pad for your skull."

As they prepared to climb up to the mouth of the cave, Joe said, "You scouted this area already?"

"Right. Earlier this summer, I went all over these parts."

"Did you hear about coal companies buying up property?"

Spencer gave Joe a guarded look.

"Seems like the stakes are pretty high," Joe said.

"Folks around here are extra protective of their privacy, especially when it comes to land, and who's buying and selling," Spencer replied.

"Why?" Joe pressed. "What have any of them got to hide?"

"Who knows and who cares?" Spencer said. "It's none of our business. I wouldn't get involved in any land politics or family feuds with these country folks. Consider Buddy's little ambush a warning."

"So that's all you know about it?" Joe said.

"Look, forget it, will you? Let's just get our work started," Spencer said. He started to climb the cliff, and Joe followed.

When they got to the ledge overlooking their campsite, Spencer popped open his oblong suitcase and pulled out a shotgun barrel and its stock, fitting the two pieces together and locking them down with a metallic snap.

"I thought we weren't supposed to have guns on this expedition," Joe said.

"This?" Spencer said. "It's just a tool we're going to use to create the shock. We fire both barrels into the floor of the cave, then take sonic readings from the shock-wave echoes." He pulled a twelve-volt battery and a seismograph out of a second bag. "This machine records the sonic images, which will give us a basic map of the rock underneath us down to about fifty meters. It's a good way to find underground passages."

He brushed aside the vines and entered the cave. Joe followed, finding himself in a cool, dank room. Their carbide lights didn't reach all the way to the back of the cave, but judging from the echoes their voices made, Joe guessed it was a large space—at least the size of a basketball court.

"Careful, the floor's slippery," Spencer said.

"Is that moss?" Joe asked, feeling his boot sink into something soft.

"Nope," Spencer replied. "That's guano."

"Guano?" Joe said.

Spencer paused, a strange grin on his face. Slowly he pointed up at the ceiling. Joe shined his helmet lantern straight up. He saw a scalloped, dome-shaped ceiling about twenty feet above their heads. For a second Joe thought someone had glued brown carpeting to the ceiling. Looking closer, he saw that the woolly mass was moving.

A dropping fell through the beam of his light, hitting him on the shoulder.

Now that his eyes were adjusting to the dark, Joe could see thousands of little heads, squeezed together, all staring down at him.

"Bats," Spencer said, following his gaze. "Probably tens of thousands of them. They're terrific creatures, but right now, we're standing in their cesspool."

"Yuck," Joe said. "Let's get out of here."

"They cluster up close to the cave mouth," Spencer said. "It's a lot cleaner at the back of this chamber. Come on."

Spencer set up the shock imager near the rear wall of the chamber. He unfolded an aluminum frame, expanding its legs into a tripod. He fitted the shotgun into the frame with its muzzle pointed downward and loaded a pair of shells into each barrel.

Next, he fixed two sensors—rubber-padded disks attached by wire to the seismograph—to the rocky floor. After hooking up the battery, he turned it on to see if it worked.

"See?" he said, showing Joe how the needles were steady until he stamped his foot next to one of the sensors. Joe watched as the needle trembled slightly.

"Once I fire the gun, the shock waves will be a lot bigger," Spencer said. "The differing intensity of the echo gives us a three-dimensional map of the rock."

"Looks like those bats are scheduled for a little wake-up call," Joe said.

"They'll get over it," Spencer said. "Ready?"

"Fire away," Joe said, covering his ears.

The blast echoed like thunder in the enclosed space, rattling Joe's chest and making his ears ring. It rocked the floor of the cavern, too, and suddenly a huge crack opened under the tripod and zigzagged its way out from where they were standing. The whole slab of rock under Joe tilted radically, then dropped into the hole.

Joe felt his stomach leap up into his throat as he slid into the black pit that had opened up under his feet.

Chapter

4

JOE TOOK A SOLID BLOW to his left elbow as he slid and let out an involuntary yelp of pain. He landed on his side, rolled a couple of feet, and bumped up against a rock wall. Rubble came pelting down on his chest and face.

He spat dust, then groaned. He touched his elbow gingerly, then he bent it slowly, wincing in pain. Well, at least it wasn't broken, he thought.

He sat up, shining his light around, and saw he was in a narrow passageway. There was a jagged hole about fifteen feet above his head. "Spencer?" he said. "If this is your idea of a joke . . ." His voice echoed eerily in the cavern.

When he stood up, he was so dizzy that he

had to brace himself against the wall. "Spencer?" he called out again. No answer.

He was reaching for a stone to throw up through the hole when a hand emerged from the pile of rubble next to him. "Spencer?" he said again. He started to pull rocks away as an arm, then a shoulder, appeared.

Lugo wasn't moving, but he was breathing. Joe uncovered his face and chest. His miner's helmet had been knocked off.

The pulse at his neck was strong and regular, and his skin didn't feel cold or clammy, which meant he probably wasn't going into shock. "Hey, Spencer, are you all right?" Joe said. "Wake up."

Lugo's eyelids fluttered, and he let out a faint groan.

Just then Joe heard Dr. Beasley's voice calling down from above. "What happened?" A light appeared, shining down through the hole. "Can you hear me?"

"I hear you," Joe replied.

"Where's Spencer?"

"Down here," Joe said. "Unconscious." There was a second groan from the graduate student. "But I think he's coming around."

"I'm rigging up a drop line," Beasley said. "Just hang on a couple of seconds. Don't move him."

Joe saw a bruise forming just above Spencer's

eye. Spencer reached up slowly and touched the wound, flinched, and dropped his arm back down.

"What happened?" Spencer murmured.

"We fell. Just stay where you are," Joe said. "Dr. Beasley's dropping us a line."

Joe heard the soft *thwack* of the rope hitting the floor behind him. Then he heard Frank yell down, "Joe, are you all right?"

"Fine," Joe called back.

"We just got back to the campsite with the rest of the equipment when we saw all these bats fly out of the cave," Frank said. "We figured something was up."

Joe's helmet light revealed the silhouette of Dr. Beasley sliding down the guide rope. Frank followed as soon as Beasley was clear.

Beasley came over and checked Spencer out. "I don't think anything's broken," he said. "Do you remember what happened?"

"I think so," Spencer said. "I fired the shock imager, and the floor just opened up."

Beasley surveyed the rubble piled around them. He shined his light on the walls of the cavern. It was a narrow corridor, with smooth, scalloped walls.

"Looks like this was some kind of waterway," Frank said.

"Definitely. It's an old river channel," Beasley replied, impressed by Frank's knowledge.

"That scalloping is the giveaway. It took thousands of years for the water to carve out that pattern."

Frank looked over the pile of stones that had fallen. "Looks like the floor was just a few inches thick in that spot," he said.

"Right, and it's all brittle limestone," Dr. Beasley agreed. "The blast must have pulverized a weak spot."

"And just like magic," Joe said, "a basement."

Suddenly Beasley became distracted. He stood stock-still and lifted his head, a puzzled expression forming on his face. He started sniffing the air.

Then Frank smelled it, too, a strange odor, not very strong, like wet moss. He put out his hand and felt a cool wet breeze, like a sprinkle of mist.

"It's just like he said," Frank said.

"Who said?" Joe asked.

"Pop McCall. He said you could smell Cathedral Cave down here."

Beasley swiveled around, facing in the direction from which the light breeze came. Ahead of him, a tunnel sloped down and off to the right.

"You fellows stay here," he said. "I'll be right back." He started to walk down the corridor, following his nose.

"Don't let him get out of sight," Joe said to

Frank. "I'll stay here with Spencer." Frank nodded wordlessly, following Beasley as he disappeared around the bend.

The tunnel narrowed, and Frank felt as if the walls were closing in on him. He had to stoop low to avoid hitting his head. As he rounded the bend, he found Beasley crouched beside a big hole. It was about seven feet across, stretching from one side of the tunnel to the other. Frank leaned over the edge, shining his light down into it. He couldn't see the bottom, but he could feel the moist air flowing up.

"Pop's right," Beasley said, grinning in the glare of Frank's carbide lantern. "What you're smelling is the center of the earth, my boy. That is one deep hole."

"Are we going down there?" Frank said.

"We'll have to anchor a rope up here somehow," Beasley said, checking around for a spot. "The question is, how long should it be?"

Frank picked up a loose stone near his foot and with a nod of approval from Beasley, dropped it into the hole. The two listened carefully for it to hit bottom. Five seconds, ten seconds, twenty, twenty-five. They never heard it hit bottom.

"Do you realize what this means?" Beasley said.

"What what means?" They heard Spencer's voice echoing from the corridor behind them.

"I told him to stay put," Joe said. "But he wouldn't."

"I'm fine," Spencer said. "A little banged up but, as Dr. Beasley said, nothing's broken. So what's all the excitement about here?"

"It looks like a breakthrough," Beasley replied. "No telling how far down it goes, but it's definitely deeper than anything else on our maps."

"So maybe it was worth a few bruises," Lugo said.

"I hope so. Let's head back to camp and rest up," Beasley said. "We'll come back here tomorrow and take some measurements."

They all trooped back to the rope, and ascended it one by one. It was twilight by the time they emerged from the mouth of the cave. Debbie and the Gallagher twins had set up the tents and started a fire in the clearing at the base of the cliff by the stream.

"I'm starved," Spencer said.

"Me, too," Joe said. "What's for dinner."

"The entrée this evening is dehydrated meat with oatmeal, sir," Alex Gallagher said. "And for dessert, we can offer a choice of shortbread biscuits or dried fruit."

"I was counting on a cheese steak sandwich with the works and then a hot fudge sundae," Joe said. "But I'll settle."

Just then Buddy McCall emerged from the

woods, clambering over a dead tree trunk and scaling down the side of the hill to the campsite. "Howdy," he said. "I came out to see how y'all were getting along." He glanced at the five tents, neatly pegged to the soil, and the well banked fire. "Looks like you got dinner going. Mind if I join you?"

"Our pleasure," Debbie said. "We were just about to dig in. I'm sure there's enough."

"Definitely," Pat Gallagher said. "It'll be ready in a jiffy."

The group settled down around the campfire to enjoy their dinner. Joe sat alongside Buddy, who leaned against a driftwood log the Gallagher twins had dragged up from the creek bank. Frank joined Debbie on one of the sleeping bags laid out on the ground.

"I have some bad news," Buddy said. "Pop took a turn for the worse today. The doctor's with him now." He paused for a moment, then said quietly, "She told me I'd better start calling the relatives because she doesn't think he'll last too much longer."

"I'm sorry to hear that," Frank said.

"Do you have any brothers or sisters?" Debbie asked.

"Just my kid brother, Dirk," Buddy replied. "He lives in Cave City. He said he'd come by in the morning."

Spencer had changed into jeans and a flannel

shirt and was crouching by the fire, poking its glowing embers with a stick.

"So it's just the two of you? No other relatives?" he said.

"That's it," Buddy replied. "And Dirk ain't lived here since he was eighteen. He and my daddy never could get along."

"So when your dad passes on, you two inherit all the land?" Spencer continued.

"Spencer," Debbie said. "That's not exactly any of our business."

"Hey, the way land speculation has been going around here," he replied, "I figured I'd just be the first to ask."

"Ain't that the truth," Buddy said. "If Pop dies, I guess them fellows from the bank is going to be circling like a bunch of vultures." He spat with disgust. "But as long as me and my brother can make payments, whoever wants the land will have to deal with us first."

"Can't the state park do something?" Frank asked.

"That's what I'm here for," Debbie replied. "If we can find a link to Cathedral Cave, then the state park could protect the land over it as a natural resource forever. There's something called a restrictive covenant the owner can sign, which prevents any kind of commercial use of a property."

Frank caught Joe's eyes at the mention of the

covenant. Either Debbie didn't know Pop had one ready or if she did she wasn't letting on.

"But if there's no link," Spencer interjected, "then the land is worthless to the park."

"Right," Debbie said.

"We'll find it," Dr. Beasley said.

"What if we find something else down there?" Frank said. "Like coal?"

"That would be bad news for the state park," Debbie said. "Kentucky Coal and Shale already has large land holdings all along our northern border. We consider them to be hostile."

"Why?" Joe asked.

"Their mining disrupts our underground ecosystem," Debbie said. "Not just at the local mine, but for miles around."

"That's not exactly true," Dr. Beasley said. "If you're strip-mining, yes, there's definitely ecosystem destruction. But strip-mining near state parks has been outlawed since 1978. And the kind of tunneling they're doing now keeps underground pollution to a minimum."

"That sounds like coal company propaganda," Debbie said. "Whose side are you on, anyway?"

"I'm a scientist and I'm neutral," Beasley said. "If there's a responsible way to exploit natural resources, then why not do it?"

"Hold it right there, Nick," Debbie said.

"Don't tell me you're moonlighting for the coal companies."

"Well, I used to do some prospecting for them," he said, "but that was before I got a permanent job at the university."

"Did you ever work for Kentucky Coal and Shale?" she said. "Those slimebags."

"Somebody's got to do it," Beasley said. "I needed the money."

"If I'd known that I would never have gotten involved with this expedition," Debbie said. "I ought to—"

"Now, you hold on for a second, Deborah," Beasley said, an edge creeping into his voice. "I haven't worked for any coal company in years. I don't have anything to do with them anymore. And I've had this argument too many times before. If you don't like it, you're free to leave. Case closed."

"Y'all sound like them protesters on TV," Buddy said. "Always haggling about some matter of principle. All I know is that whatever happens I'm staying on this land. It's been in our family for five generations, and it's gonna stay that way.

"I'm gonna go check on my daddy. Y'all have a good night. Git some rest and stop your fussin' and fightin'."

Later that night, as Frank and Joe climbed into their tent and settled into their sleeping bags, Frank said, "Beasley sure clammed up when Debbie lit into him about being a coal prospector."

"She's not exactly Miss Charming," Joe said. "I'll bet she gave Pop that covenant, and now that he's sick she'll be pressuring him to sign."

"Looks like it's going to come down to a contest between her and whoever's secretly working for the coal company," Frank said.

"Do you think it's Beasley?" Joe said.

"Could be. He's the head of the expedition, so it's hard to question his orders. He can pretty much get away with what he wants."

"How about Lugo?" Joe asked. "Buddy shows up to tell us his father might die, and the guy's already quizzing him about who's going to inherit the land. And this afternoon I was just trying to make conversation and he told me to mind my own business."

"As Dad said, let's just keep an eye on everybody and try to sort out who's doing what," Frank said with a yawn.

The brothers drifted off to sleep, listening to the all-night music of the buzzing crickets and the hooting owls.

Sometime early the next morning the wind picked up, disturbing Frank's dreams. He woke with a start as the sky was starting to lighten. Before he could shake the cobwebs out of his

head, he caught a whiff of something strange—
like burning plastic.

He unzipped the door of their tent and
peered out. The campsite seemed still and silent.
But then something caught his eye: it was a
small column of smoke rising up beside Dr.
Beasley's tent.

Before Frank could react, a scream pierced
the still air and Beasley came running out of
his tent, clawing at his pajama legs, which were
flickering with flames.

Chapter

5

BEASLEY SPRINTED THE TWENTY FEET to the edge of the stream and jumped in feet first. Frank scrambled out of his tent and ran to the stream. By the time he got there Beasley was standing waist deep in water.

"Are you okay?" Frank said.

"I think so," Beasley replied in a shaky voice.

Frank glanced over his shoulder at Beasley's test, which was engulfed in flames. Joe was throwing handfuls of sand onto it with the Gallagher twins. The tent was burning fast.

As Dr. Beasley waded out of the stream, Frank could see that all the hair had been singed off his legs and angry red splotches were forming on the skin around his kneecaps.

45

"Looks like first-degree burns," Frank said. "Better keep them in cool water. It'll help take some of the heat out until we can get you to a hospital."

"I'm not going to any hospital," Beasley said. "First-degree burns aren't any worse than a bad sunburn. If they blister, I'll just put some first-aid cream on them."

Frank glanced back at the campsite and noticed that Spencer had emerged from his tent. He, Joe, and the twins were standing over the remains of Beasley's tent—a blackened jumble of scraps. Debbie's tent was still zipped up tight.

"Who banked that fire last night?" Frank asked.

"I guess it was Debbie," Beasley said.

"The embers must have blown up against the tent," Frank said. "It was pretty breezy."

Frank went over to Debbie's tent. He didn't notice anything unusual at first. Looking closer, he saw that the nylon fabric around the tent's zipper was smeared with ashes from the campfire.

"Knock, knock," Joe said, coming up to the tent. "Debbie, are you in there?"

They heard her turn over in her sleeping bag, and then her voice, thick with sleep, muttered, "Wha—" She fumbled with the tent zipper and stuck her head out, squinting. "What's up?" she asked, stifling a yawn.

"Somebody may have set fire to Dr. Beasley's tent," Frank said.

Debbie paused for the words to sink in. "Is he all right?" she asked as she crawled out of her tent.

"He is, but it was close," Frank replied.

"What's that stuff smudged on your tent?" Joe asked.

"I don't know," she said. "Looks like dirt."

"It's ashes from the fire," Joe said. "Did you get up last night?"

She hesitated. Before she could answer, Lugo said, "She sure did. I heard her. I don't know what time it was, but I heard her come out here by the fire."

"Around midnight I did get up," she said. "I couldn't sleep and I guess I was still angry at Dr. Beasley for not telling me about working for Kentucky Coal and Shale."

"So you figured you'd make things a little hot for him?" Joe said.

"Excuse me," Debbie said, "but do I hear you accusing me of arson?"

"I just wondered how you account for the ashes on your tent door," Joe said. "And for this." He held up a straight length of smoldering branch about twenty inches long and several inches thick. "I found it shoved under Dr. Beasley's tent."

"Look, Sherlock Holmes," she said angrily, "you'd better back off. I didn't set any fire. Did it occur to you that the ashes got there because I banked the fire and didn't wash my hands afterward? And how do you know that stick was burning before somebody supposedly shoved it under the tent? Do you seriously think I'd be so stupid as to set Dr. Beasley's tent on fire like that?"

Joe would have been happy to argue the point, but he was interrupted by Buddy, who walked into the clearing still wearing his clothes from the night before. He looked as if he hadn't slept at all. His expression was grief stricken. "Pop died about four hours ago," he said.

"I'm so sorry," Joe said.

"That's terrible," Frank said. "What happened?"

Buddy hung his head. "I didn't think he felt a thing. His heart seized up. It all happened in a couple of seconds. He just slipped away—right in front of my eyes."

Dr. Beasley, with his pajama bottoms hanging in charred wet strips below his knees, put a hand on Buddy's shoulder. "Is there anything we can do for you?"

Buddy heaved a sigh and shook his head. "My brother's coming soon."

"I can help out with the funeral arrangements," Debbie said.

"We can all help," Joe said.

"That'd be nice," Buddy replied. "I just don't like being in that cabin all alone."

Debbie ducked back into her tent to throw

on some more clothes, then led Buddy back up the trail to his cabin.

"I can't believe it," Frank said. "Mr. McCall didn't seem that sick yesterday afternoon, at least not when we were talking."

The group fell silent for a few minutes. Finally Dr. Beasley spoke. "I'm going to need something to wear. Most of what I had was in that tent."

"You can borrow some of my clothes," Joe said.

"Thanks," Dr. Beasley replied. "I can run into town to buy some."

"We'd like to go up to the cabin and pay our respects," Frank said after Beasley had changed.

"Pat and Alex can stay here with me, and we'll clean up this mess," Spencer said.

"All right. I should be back early this afternoon," Beasley said.

They trudged up through the woods in silence, each lost in his own thoughts. Before they reached the cabin, Beasley said, "I don't think Pop would want us to call off the expedition."

"No, I think he'd want us to get down there and start exploring," Frank said.

When they got to the cabin, there was a late-model luxury sedan parked in the driveway next to Debbie's four-by-four truck. Joe stopped to admire the sleek vehicle.

"I wonder whose it is," Frank said.

"Probably has something to do with the funeral," Beasley suggested. "I'm not going to disturb them in the cabin. Would you please tell them I'll be back in a couple of hours?"

Frank watched as Beasley started up the university van and drove slowly down the steep road toward the highway. Then he turned to follow Joe up the steps to the house.

"Anybody home?" Joe called through the screen door. No answer. He entered the living room, where a sagging couch piled with blankets faced a vintage black-and-white television set. The room was littered with unwashed dishes, half-empty pill bottles, and outdated magazines.

"Where is everybody?" Joe said.

"Shh," Frank said. "Let's show a little respect." He shouldered past his brother and entered the hallway, glancing into the first room he saw.

Pop McCall's body had been laid out on the bed. His hands had been folded across his chest, and his hair was combed neatly. Debbie was sitting in a chair at the foot of the bed. She had obviously been crying.

Joe came up behind Frank and started to say something, but when he caught sight of the old man's body on the bed, he fell silent.

After a few moments Debbie stood and went into the living room, Frank and Joe following.

She sighed heavily. "It's such a shame," she

said. "People around here struggle in poverty all their lives, barely surviving. And for what? To see everything they have taken from them?"

"I just wish I'd had a chance to tell him the cave smelled just the way he said it would," Frank said.

"What's Buddy going to do now?" Joe asked. "I guess they were pretty close."

"That's what he and Dirk are talking about," Debbie answered. "That's Dirk's car out in the driveway. He was here when we got back. They went down to the family graveyard to pick out a spot to bury their father.

"I ought to make some phone calls," she said. "They want to hold the service right away— this afternoon."

Debbie went to the back of the house and Frank joined Joe at the window overlooking the driveway. He glanced at the table where he'd seen the restrictive covenant document the day before. It was gone now. "I wonder if he signed it," Frank said, "before he—"

"Hey, who's that?" Joe said. There was a man wearing a double-breasted blue suit and shiny black cowboy boots striding out of the woods.

Buddy emerged behind him. "Must be Dirk," Joe said in a whisper. Frank could see the resemblance to Pop and Buddy in the man's prominent chin and square forehead, but the similarities stopped there. His city-slicker image was miles from Buddy's beard, flannel shirt, and overalls.

The two came within hearing distance, standing just behind the window. Frank and Joe stepped back behind the curtains, but they could hear Buddy loud and clear. He sounded angry. "You should show some respect. Any bad blood between you two is over. He's dead, Dirk. Can't you just leave it at that?"

"Forget it," Dirk replied. "The sooner he's in the ground, the better. If it were up to me, I wouldn't even bury him in the family plot. He doesn't deserve it. I'd just as soon leave him out in the woods for the birds to feed on. Serve him right after what he did to me."

"Shut up, little brother," Buddy warned. "We marked out the plot, and that's where he's going to be buried."

"It's just a boneyard anyway," Dirk said. "When I sell my land, whoever buys it ain't going to care about a bunch of old hillbilly headstones."

"Sell out?" Buddy said. "You can't do that."

"Who says I can't," Dirk said. "You think I'd want to hold on to this land when I could get a load of cash for it?"

Buddy glared silently at his brother. "You're not one of us anymore, with your big-city ways. Just like when you drove that old truck up here, parkin' it under the house and sellin' them tires. You just got no respect."

"Always the same old story," Dirk said. "Well, you can keep on whining and crying like a broken-down old hillbilly, but I'm gonna git me a life. See, I already leased this new car on credit. Same goes for this suit and these boots. They're real—"

He never finished his sentence because Buddy shoved him hard against the hood of the car. "You greedy little weasel," he shouted.

Dirk was so quick with the knife that Joe didn't see where he drew it from. He only saw the bright glint of the blade and the blur of his hand as he swiped the air inches from Buddy's face.

Buddy was fast for a big man, though. He jumped back, crouched down, and said, "So that's the way it's gonna be, huh? Just like when Daddy kicked you out of the house the first time. You gonna cut me, too?" He stooped to pick up a tire iron that lay near his foot. "Okay, weasel, come and get me."

Dirk circled slowly, poised to strike. "Come on, Buddy," he said in a menacing voice. "I've been waitin' for this chance for years." He tossed the knife to his left hand. "Let's finish this once and for all."

Dirk feinted left, then leaped at his big brother, knife flashing.

Chapter

6

FRANK AND JOE flew out the screen door and took the steps down to the driveway two at a time just as Buddy swung the tire iron in a vicious arc, connecting with Dirk's forehead.

Dirk went down, and Buddy stood over him, trembling with rage. He raised the tire iron high, ready to smash Dirk again, but Joe caught his wrist while Frank grabbed the big man's other arm and held him still with a half nelson.

"Back off," Joe shouted. "He's hurt." He loosed Buddy's grip on the tire iron, and it fell to the dirt.

"Good-for-nothing," Buddy snarled. "He ain't even worth spittin' on. He never had no respect for Pop or anybody else."

Frank let Buddy go and bent down to examine Dirk and take his vital signs. "Out cold," he said. There was a nasty gash splitting his eyebrow, and blood trickled down his temple to his ear.

Buddy was still struggling against Joe's grip. "Get a hold of yourself," Joe said. "It's over." He tossed Buddy's arm down, and only then did he notice the big man was hurt, too.

"You're cut," Joe said. "Sit down." Buddy's shirt was split open over his upper arm and there was a deep gash in his bicep. His sleeve was soaked in blood to the elbow.

Buddy glanced down at the wound, then glowered at his brother. "Pipsqueak," he muttered. "I thought he missed me by a mile."

Joe quickly unfastened his belt and looped it around Buddy's arm, tightening it into a tourniquet at the armpit.

"Hold this tight," Joe told Buddy. "It should stop the bleeding."

They heard Debbie Cameron's voice behind them. "What's going on out here?"

"Call an ambulance," Frank said. "Quick."

"No," Buddy roared. "You ain't callin' nobody."

"Hold still," Joe said. "You're gonna—"

"Shut up," Buddy said, elbowing Joe aside with his good arm. "Debbie, you stay put. *I* say what happens around here. And nobody's gonna call no ambulance."

He was standing up now, holding the tourniquet on his arm tight. Joe noticed his knees were wobbly and he was sweating a lot. Was he going to fall down? Or maybe he'd try to go after Dirk again.

"He's coming around," Frank said, still bending over Dirk.

"Let me take a look at that cut," Debbie said to Buddy.

"He should see a doctor," Joe said. "He's going to need stitches."

"That's not the way they do things around here," she replied. She inspected Buddy's arm. "Get on upstairs, Buddy," she said. "Get out some rubbing alcohol. I'm going to need a needle and thread, too. And boiling water to sterilize them. You got a sewing kit?"

Joe was surprised to see Buddy nod his head. As he turned to go up to the cabin, still holding the strap on his arm, Debbie grabbed his good arm and said, "Buddy, you know this isn't the way to go about settling family feuds."

"Yep, I do," he said, his voice was softer now. "It's just that he—"

"It doesn't matter who started it," she interrupted. "What matters is how you finish it. Let's hope it's peacefully. You've both done enough damage for one day."

"What do you think of this one, Doc?" Frank asked, jerking his thumb in Dirk's direction.

"Well, I'm not exactly a doctor, but I do have some training in emergency field medicine," she said. She peered closely at Dirk's cut. "Dirk here has quite a reputation in Cave City. He's a born scrapper. When he was a teenager he got caught spray-painting graffiti on the walls of Cathedral Cave. A real Kentucky rebel. It's not in my job description, but you'd be surprised how many family squabbles I've had to mop up after."

She inspected Dirk's pupils. "The eyes look fine. Dirk, can you hear me?" He groaned, then licked his lips. "Don't talk, just lie still. You're going to be all right. Do you remember what happened?"

Dirk swallowed. Frank could see him struggling to form words, but he merely nodded.

"Good," Debbie said. "I think he'll be okay. Let's carry him inside, guys, and I'll clean him up."

Within an hour, Debbie had Buddy's wound stitched up. With no pain killers other than aspirin, it must have really hurt, but Buddy had just grunted each time Debbie used the needle to close the wound. The finished job was crude, but it would heal—and probably leave an impressive looking scar.

Now she was ready to start on Dirk. She cleaned the cut on his eyebrow and said, "I can close that up with adhesive strips. But you're going to have a scar, too."

Just then Dr. Beasley opened the screen door and came into the living room. Frank noticed he was wearing a pair of new overalls and a cotton shirt. He was carrying the clothes he had borrowed from Joe.

"What happened?" he said when he saw the blood-stained cloth in Debbie's hand.

Frank told him about the fight. "Maybe we ought to call this whole expedition off," he said. "Conditions don't seem right for a team—"

"No way," Buddy said. "Now that Pop is gone, it's more important than ever to find that link."

"What're you talkin' about?" Dirk said.

"These folks made a deal with Pop," Buddy explained. "It don't have nothin' to do with you."

"It does, too," Dirk replied. Shoving Debbie's hand away, he sat up. "He's dead now. And I stand to inherit half of this land. So it *is* my business." He looked at Beasley. "Go on, mister. Let's hear about your expedition."

Beasley briefed Dirk on their goals and their finds so far, and when he was done, Dirk asked, "How many of you are there?"

"Seven in all," Dr. Beasley said. "Two surface support staff, plus five deep cave explorers."

"You must have room for one more," Dirk said. "I got plenty of time. I ain't been on a caving expedition in about six years, but I had plenty of background before that."

"I don't know," Dr. Beasley said carefully. "That would depend on your—"

"Shouldn't we talk about this after the funeral?" Debbie interrupted.

"That's right," Buddy said. "Let's bury Pop first, and then y'all can talk business. I've arranged for the pastor to say a service in about two hours."

"Frank, Joe, why don't you go dig a grave, and I'll keep my eyes on those two," Debbie said, nodding over her shoulder at Buddy and Dirk.

"I hope they can get along well enough to nail together a coffin while we're gone," Frank said as he and Joe picked up a couple of picks and shovels from a shed and headed into the woods.

The air was hot and humid. They followed Buddy's directions to the family graveyard, a half mile into the woods. They found a plot staked out with birch branches. A few crudely carved headstones marked the other graves.

At first Frank and Joe worked in silence, stripped to their waists and sweating in the oppressive heat. Joe used a pickax to break up the flinty topsoil while Frank heaved big shovelfuls into a pile next to the grave.

"Luckily they didn't kill each other," Joe said finally, pausing to rest. "Spencer warned me to stay out of any family feuds between these people. Now I'm beginning to see what he was talking about. Those two don't pull any punches."

Frank's jaw was set, and he kept on digging. Joe recognized that look of intense concentration and realized that Frank probably hadn't heard a word he'd said.

"Earth to Frank, Earth to Frank," Joe said. "Come in, Frank. What's going on up there?"

Frank looked up in surprise, then frowned. "I was just wondering about Debbie."

"You mean whether she was actually angry enough to set Beasley's tent on fire?" Joe said.

"I don't see it," Frank said. "It just reeks of a frame job to me."

"Right, and don't forget the acid on the rope," Joe said. "I wonder who arranged that 'accident.'"

"The question is," Frank said, "who's trying to sabotage the expedition, and why?"

"Who would stand to gain if Beasley was killed?" Joe said.

"Nobody, really, which is why I'm stumped," Frank said. "If they find a link to Cathedral Cave, then Debbie gets to protect the land from

Kentucky Coal and Shale. If they find coal down there, then the land'll be a lot more valuable, which would benefit Dirk and Buddy."

Frank took a long look at the hole they were digging, then scooped up another shovelful of dirt. "Poor old Pop McCall," he said. "None of it matters to him anymore. Too bad. He seemed really excited about having a bunch of cavers around."

"Let's have a talk with Buddy after the funeral," Joe said. "Just to make sure he knows we're on his side. Then maybe he can help clear some of this up."

"Sounds good," Frank said. They dug for another twenty minutes in silence. Then Joe stopped shoveling, mopped his brow, and said, "Looks like at least six feet. That should do it. Let's head back and get something to drink."

The two trudged back through the woods. Frank was lost in thought again, trailing a few steps behind Joe. A hundred yards from the house, Joe glanced ahead and caught a flash of bright red fabric through the tangled underbrush. He motioned to Frank, and they both froze in their tracks, crouching just off the path. They could see somebody in a red T-shirt standing off in the woods about fifty yards ahead.

"Lugo," Joe whispered.

Frank saw the stocky graduate student talking to another man—Dirk McCall. They were too far away to pick out any words, but Spencer was speaking quickly as Dirk nodded his head gravely.

"Strange," Joe said in a low whisper. "I didn't realize those two even knew each other." Joe shifted his position and must have stepped on a dry twig because there was a loud snap.

At the sound Dirk stopped talking and scanned the woods. "Who's that?" he yelled. "Who's out there?"

Chapter

7

THE INSTANT DIRK YELLED OUT, Frank and Joe stepped back onto the path and headed noisily back to the cabin. Dirk caught up with them halfway there. Spencer was nowhere in sight.

"Hey, you guys sure came out of nowhere," Dirk said. "You didn't see anybody else back there in the woods, did you? I thought I heard somebody."

"Nope, we didn't see anybody or anything," Frank said. "We were just heading back to the house. Where were you?"

"Oh, just out for a walk," Dirk said. "I guess I needed some time alone. Everything okay? You two finished digging my daddy's grave?"

"Yes, sir, we did," Joe said.

"I really do appreciate that," Dirk said. "I guess we can get this thing over with now."

When the Hardys got back to the cabin Spencer was waiting for them. Frank noticed beads of sweat on his temples. He must have hustled around the long way, Frank thought, while Dirk took the path to intercept them.

Frank also noticed that Lugo and Dirk didn't even acknowledge each other. Their meeting was definitely top secret, and there wasn't any point in questioning them about it. It would put them on guard, and they'd just deny it ever happened. Besides, the pastor had already arrived. He was a skinny, haggard-looking older man with a sour expression.

The pastor immediately stepped forward to greet Dirk. With Dr. Beasley, Buddy, Debbie, and the Gallagher twins gathered, the funeral procession was ready to begin. The pastor had Dirk and Buddy lead the pallbearers. Frank and Joe followed them with the twins at the rear. The six of them hoisted the simple plywood coffin and, with solemn steps, the small group of mourners picked its way along the wooded trail.

At the grave site, the pastor read a few words from the Bible. Frank watched Dirk and Spencer for signs of communication during the service, but they both kept their eyes on the coffin. In fact, Frank could imagine that Dirk was genuinely grieving his father's death. Pretty soon he realized it was all an act, though.

As the party was heading back to the cabin, Dirk said to Beasley, "So what do you say to me joining your little underground expedition?"

"I've been thinking about that," Dr. Beasley said, frowning. "And I've decided against it."

"Sorry, but I'm going along," Dirk replied. "You just try to stop me."

"Well, *I'm* sorry," Beasley said, "but the contract stipulates—"

"You mean this contract?" Dirk said, pulling a crumpled piece of paper out of his pocket. Frank recognized the rental agreement he'd seen inside the cabin. "I declare any contract null and void," Dirk said, ripping it in half, "on account of the signer's being dead."

He turned to Debbie. "And as for your restricted convent or whatever you're callin' it, you can just forget it." He pulled out the second document and tore that in half, too.

"You just don't have any idea what you're doing, do you?" Debbie said.

"Is that so?" Dirk said. "Well, I ain't so dumb as you think, and I know when someone's trying to take what ain't rightfully theirs."

Frank could tell Debbie was struggling to control her anger. Finally she said, "There just isn't any room for you on this expedition. We don't have enough supplies or equipment."

"Don't you worry your pretty head 'bout that," Dirk replied. "I'll use my daddy's equipment."

"This is a scientific expedition," Debbie said. "Not a joy ride."

Dirk scowled. "I don't have to take your lip. I'm half owner of this here land. Either you let me come with you or nobody goes down there."

"What do you say, Spencer?" Joe said in a half whisper to Lugo. "Should Dirk come along?"

Spencer shrugged. "Doesn't make any difference to me," he said. "Dr. Beasley's the boss. I do whatever he says."

Everyone turned to look at Dr. Beasley, who was shifting uncomfortably. He glanced at Buddy. The man's face still registered grief from the funeral. "This is between Buddy and Dirk," he said. "They own the land now."

Buddy glanced contemptuously at Dirk. "I don't care what he does," he said. "Just as long as I don't have to clean up after him anymore." He turned to go back into the cabin.

"So it's settled, then," Dirk said. "I'll see you all tomorrow morning at the cave mouth."

Nobody said much on the way back to the campsite. The Gallagher twins fixed macaroni and cheese for dinner, and everyone ate in silence. Frank and Joe decided to turn in early.

"Dirk's a real loser," Joe said, once he and Frank were settled into their sleeping bags. "I can't believe Dr. Beasley is letting him in on the expedition."

Frank shook his head. "I know. I've got a feeling this could get ugly," he said.

"You think so?" Joe asked.

"You saw how angry Debbie was," Frank said, "not to mention Dr. Beasley losing his contract. I wonder if Dirk realizes he's going underground with a bunch of people who would just as soon he never comes back up."

"Remember, he's a scrapper," Joe said.

"All I know is we'd better be on the lookout for more 'accidents,' " Frank said.

"On the bright side," Joe said, "this is the perfect chance to keep an eye on *everybody*."

"Except Buddy," Frank said.

"Right, except Buddy," Joe said.

It seemed like only seconds after Joe closed his eyes that Beasley unzipped their tent to wake them up. The sun was just peeking over the ridge. Breakfast consisted of granola and soy milk. Once everyone finished eating, Beasley instructed them to assemble their caving gear.

"The Gallagher twins are going to stay up here on the surface," he said. "They're our lifeline." He turned to the twins. "After we go in, I want you two to ferry all the equipment we can't carry down to the base camp. Set up the cooking equipment, organize the supplies. While you're doing that, we'll be exploring deeper into the cavern."

Just then Dirk appeared, wearing a pair of mud-stained coveralls that looked as if they belonged to a car mechanic. Around his waist was a rubber inner tube, deflated and cut into a half-doughnut shape, full of tools. Frank could see a ball peen hammer, a chisel, and a collection of rusty-looking clips and stakes. On his back Dirk wore a canvas pack. For a helmet he used a beat-up construction worker's hard hat with a flashlight taped to the crown.

Beasley took one look at Dirk's equipment and mumbled, "Primitive," under his breath. Then he turned to the group and announced, "All right everybody, let's go."

One by one they climbed the cliff and went inside the cave. Joe hustled underneath the bat colony—he'd seen enough of them already—but Frank and the others stopped to look up at the thousands of pairs of eyes staring down from the ceiling.

Joe went straight over to the jagged hole in the floor. He took the rope down, and the others followed. Within minutes, they were all clustered around the deep chasm Beasley had discovered two days before. Once again they could feel the damp cave wind blowing gently up from the hole.

"It's seven hundred fifty feet down," Lugo reported, showing them the anchor rope he'd fixed there after the funeral the day before.

This was going to be interesting, Frank thought. They were about to slide down a rope into a black hole the same height as a fifty-story building.

Beasley inspected the stakes of tempered steel pounded into crevices in the limestone and tested the knots anchoring the rope.

"We might be scrambled eggs if Dr. Beasley hadn't found that battery acid on the old set of ropes," Joe whispered to Frank.

Beasley went first. He clipped his spring-loaded cam to the rope, making sure his webbed belt and harness held his weight comfortably before swinging down into the blackness.

Joe peered over the edge as Dr. Beasley's helmet light grew smaller and smaller, finally fading from view. Frank stood beside him, listening to the rope creaking with the expedition leader's weight. Five minutes, ten minutes—it seemed like an hour before they heard a distant whistle.

"That's it," Spencer said. "He's at the bottom."

Debbie went next, with Spencer following, then Dirk.

"After you," Joe told Frank, once they heard the signal from below.

"You go ahead," Frank said.

"Might as well get it over with," Joe said. He clipped his spring-loaded cam onto the rope, testing its bite into the rope by leaning against his webbed harness. He felt the slender woven strand pass through the metal rings smoothly. With a wink at Frank, he stepped off into space.

Twirling down through the blackness, Joe felt like a spider on a thread. He half expected to bang up against solid rock any second, but the beam of his carbide light didn't reveal any walls so the passage must have been plenty wide. Gripping the rope above him, and keeping the slack rope below him feeding smoothly into the cam, he lowered himself carefully. He knew that his auto-brake cam would stop him from free falling, but if that little spring-loaded mechanism failed, he'd be like an elevator without a cable.

After almost five minutes of dropping through utter blackness, he saw three tiny pinpricks of light below him. He grew dizzy watching them twirl. By the time he reached the bottom, he was so disoriented that Dr. Beasley had to help him unhook his pack and take it off.

"Don't worry, Joe," the professor said. "You'll find your cave legs in a couple of minutes."

While Frank was descending the long rope, Beasley lit two flares, which gave off the rotten-egg odor of sulphur. The harsh light from the flares partially illuminated the cavern, and Joe was astonished by its size.

A dome arched seven hundred fifty feet above his head, studded with rocky formations and stained with water deposits. It was like being in a giant roofed football stadium, only three times larger.

Looking around, Joe saw that the floor of the cave looked like a moonscape. Cone-shaped stalagmites rose as high as his chest. Boulders as big as houses blocked their view of the entire chamber.

"Let's hustle, fellas," Beasley said as soon as Frank landed. "We have to pick out a base campsite while those flares last. That looks like a level spot over there."

"After the Gallaghers lower the rest of the supplies," Beasley said, "we should have enough to last a week. We'll just carry sleeping bags and enough food for a twenty-four-hour excursion. Then we can come back to resupply as needed."

"That should give us enough time to cross the boundary between Dismal Hollow and the state park," Spencer said. "Assuming we can find passable tunnel access that far."

Dr. Beasley checked his compass. "If we head

due southwest, we'll be on a beeline for Cathedral Cave."

"I'll fix an anchor for our guideline," Spencer said. With Dr. Beasley leading, the group moved single file through the dips and humps of the cave floor. Spencer brought up the rear, unspooling a reel of fishing line and pausing every fifty feet or so to anchor it. This and the ropes were their only way out.

As they advanced slowly, Joe caught glimpses of huge mounds of crystallized minerals, glittering fiercely in the glare of their lamps. After an hour of exploring, Beasley signaled a rest. Joe gratefully dropped his pack and sat down next to it. Following Spencer's example, he pulled out a peanut butter and jelly sandwich. He was so hungry he devoured half the sandwich in three bites.

"How far did we come?" he wondered after taking a drink of bottled water.

"Just about twenty-nine hundred yards, according to my pedometer," Spencer reported. "Six hundred yards shy of two miles."

"It's a lot lower here," Beasley said. He shined his light directly overhead, and the others followed his example. "We must be near the end of this chamber." Joe was surprised to see the ceiling less than ten feet above his head.

"Why don't we light another flare?" Beasley

suggested. "Maybe we can see the back wall from here."

Spencer took another flare out of his pack and said, "Okay, here we go." Standing several feet from the group, he struck a match and lit the flare, then wedged it in a crevice.

The sudden glare illuminated an amazing sight. Twenty yards in front of them, rising to a height of more than ten feet, was a wall pocketed with small openings. It looked like the honeycombed structures built by bees, Frank realized, but the scale was enormous.

"What is that?" Joe asked.

"I've never seen anything like it," Dr. Beasley said. He approached the honeycombed wall. "It's that cave wind again," he called out. "I can smell it and I can feel it. It's coming from over here."

The rest of the group joined him. They could smell it, too—that same damp, cloistered smell, that same cool, misty air.

"Here," Beasley said, pointing to one of the openings at chest height. "It's strongest here. I'm going in."

"It's too narrow for the packs," Spencer said.

"True," Beasley said, "but we can drag them behind us." He took off his pack and hitched it to his belt with a three-foot rope. Then he climbed into the hole head first, pulling his bundle behind him.

Spencer followed, then Dirk, then Debbie. Frank hoisted himself up next, with Joe taking up the rear.

For several dozen yards they crawled on their hands and knees. Gradually, the passageway narrowed to the point where they had to squirm on their stomachs. Joe could feel the moisture soaking through his gloves. His lantern revealed a thin stream of water trickling down the center of the tunnel, flowing from his feet forward. As they squirmed inch by inch through the tunnel, the only thing he could see ahead of him was the bottom of Frank's pack and the soles of his boots.

After twenty minutes Joe was ready to give up. "Man, I can't take much more of this," he said. Frank had stopped for a quick breather, and Joe had no choice but to wait.

"Just sit back, relax, and enjoy the view," Frank said.

"Very funny," Joe said.

"Hey, I'm sure we're almost there," Frank said.

They started crawling again. The air seemed to be getting thinner and the tunnel narrower. It was at least another ten minutes of slow going before Joe heard some muffled shouts ahead.

"Beasley found a second cavern up there," Frank said. "He said it's huge. He's standing up in it right now."

"So hurry up, let's go," Joe said. "What are we waiting for?"

Frank and Joe wriggled hard and fast over the last twenty yards. When Joe finally pulled himself out of the hole, he could feel the space open around him, even though it was pitch black. Beasley lit another flare, and the six of them stopped to admire the cavern they'd discovered.

It looked like a smaller version of the one they'd just spent almost an hour crawling from. The roof was lower, but the rock formations were equally spectacular.

Standing in front of the mouth of the tunnel, Joe could feel the cave breeze, with its strange, mossy smell. For a second he thought he heard a light rattling sound, like a wind chime made out of hollow wooden tubes. He sensed a spindly shadow out of the corner of his eye and turned toward it. When his head lamp fell full on it, Joe let out a gasp.

The hand of a human skeleton was dangling inches from his face.

Chapter

8

JOE LOOKED UP at the ledge above and froze. There was a row of human skulls staring down at him with toothy grins and empty eye sockets. He felt something brush his cheek, then jerked back, swiping at it and dashing it to the floor where it shattered into little pieces. It was the dangling skeleton hand.

At the clattering sound, the other five explorers whirled around and their lamps illuminated a ghastly sight. There were a series of ledges in the cavern wall, and on every ledge at least three dozen skeletons were staring down at them. Their gleaming white rib cages and gaping mouths glowed in the beams from the explorers' hissing carbide lamps.

"What the—" said Dirk, stepping back. Lugo let loose a low whistle, and Beasley caught his breath.

Joe stared at the pile of shattered bones at his feet and felt a powerful shudder of revulsion. With the back of his hand he wiped his cheek where the bones had brushed it.

"Stand back, everybody." Debbie's voice cracked the stunned silence like a whip. "Joe, don't move. Unless you want to wreck the whole thing."

Joe nodded and stayed put. "What is this, some kind of crypt?" he said.

"Looks like we aren't the first people ever to climb through that hole," Frank said.

"That's true," Debbie said. "But I bet it's been about thirty thousand years since the last one did." Her voice became hushed with awe. "Nick, do you realize what we're looking at?"

"I think so," Dr. Beasley said. "But you're the expert in archeology."

"It's the same burial pattern as the ones in Cathedral Cave," Debbie said. "Squatting position, with the arms crossed over the shin bones, each one leaning against the next. It's got to be the same tribe."

"Which tribe would that be?" Frank asked.

"They're prehistoric," she explained. "An extinct population, we believe. We call them the Bone People of Cathedral Cave, because all we know about them are their bones and burial rituals. They lived around the time of the last ice age." She paused. "I don't believe anyone's ever seen such a well-preserved site."

With growing enthusiasm in his voice, Beasley said, "This proves it, doesn't it? I mean, if these skeletons are the same as the ones found in Cathedral Cave, then there must be a link."

Debbie nodded. "I'd say so. But where? People have been exploring Cathedral Cave for over a hundred and fifty years, and no one's stumbled on it yet."

"I didn't realize it had been that long," Frank said.

"People have always gone after ancient artifacts like this," Debbie said. "A hundred years ago, before there were any state parks, grave robbers plundered all the skeletons in Cathedral Cave, selling them to museums and destroying the integrity of the sites." She nodded at the arrangement on the walls. "This one doesn't look like it's been touched."

"Until now," Joe said, looking down at the ancient arm bones he'd broken. "I feel bad. I guess I got a little rattled. Sorry."

"You can see how fragile this stuff is," Debbie said. "We've got to be extra careful not to stir it up."

"All right, let's get started looking for that link," Beasley said, dropping his pack. "Joe, you stay here with Debbie and take samples of the burial site while the rest of us do a little preliminary surveying."

Frank helped Beasley unpack his surveying equipment. "We'll use the mouth of the wormhole as our reference point," Beasley said. "Everything gets measured from there—the pitch, the grade, the distance. Later, I can draw a map from the coordinates we take."

While Frank planted the sighting pole, Beasley walked down the slope, playing out the tape measure to a distance of four meters. Here he took a small wax candle from his pack, lit it, and planted it. He took measurements from his compass, reading out the numbers while Frank wrote the information down on a pad of paper.

Then they leapfrogged to the next position, repeating the procedure, then leapfrogged again. Within half an hour, they were fifty yards from the wormhole, heading downhill.

Meanwhile, Joe helped Debbie take a photograph of the skeleton wall. She showed him how to take samples from around the bones without disturbing them, and then how to store the samples in self-sealing plastic bags and label them with a grease pencil.

"This kind of analysis is going the way of the dinosaurs," she explained. "I'll send these chips off to the lab where they have an X-ray spectrometer. Now, thanks to miniaturization and computer technology, we can bring the analytical tools right to the site."

Joe was listening to her explanation, but he was also keeping an eye on Dirk and Lugo. They took their surveying equipment off to the left, clinging to the wall of the roughly circular chamber. They didn't go very far, just outside of hearing range.

Joe was considering how to slip away from Debbie in order to follow them, when Beasley lit a second flare. With the intense light of the fire illuminating the entire cavern, Joe could see Frank and Beasley standing about a hundred feet downhill beside a narrow canyon that ran from one side of the chamber to the other. He heard Beasley shout, "It's a river."

Debbie turned around. "Wow, what a sight," she said, admiring the huge underground room, its floor split dramatically by a deep, swift-flowing river.

Meanwhile, Joe kept watching Dirk and Spencer, who had stopped to stare at the ceiling of the chamber. Dirk was pointing up. Most of the ceiling, which was scalloped here and there in graceful patterns, glowed a whitish color, and Joe guessed it was made of limestone. But there was a wide dark streak, too. At first Joe thought it was just a big empty crack, like a mirror image of the river crevice in the floor, but as his light played over it he could see it was a solid wedge of glittering black stone that ran the entire length of the chamber.

"I hope that's not what I think it is," Debbie muttered.

Dirk let out a long whistle that echoed all over the chamber. "Would you look at that vein!" he said. "Black gold. I do believe we just found our mother lode!"

"Not so fast, Dirk," Debbie called out. His helmet light swung around and bathed her in yellow light. She pointed at the skeletons behind her. "If that's coal, you can forget about trying to get at it. There's no way you'd get a permit to mine with a valuable find like this burial site here."

"Baloney," Dirk said. "Ain't no pile of bones going to keep me from mining my land."

"These bones are worth a lot more money in the long run," Debbie said. "This is going to be a major tourist attraction."

"Aw, c'mon," Dirk sneered. "You're talking about the difference between running a souvenir stand and living like a millionaire. Ain't no choice there."

"You're right, you don't have a choice," Debbie said. "As long as these skeletons are here, that coal is staying in the ground. And the law's behind me on this one."

Dirk didn't answer, but Joe could see a determined scowl on his face.

"Hey," Spencer said, "this is no time to argue."

"I'm goin' to take a look at my mother lode," Dirk said. "Y'all just try and stop me." He whirled around and stalked off toward the far end of the chamber where the black vein met the floor. Spencer followed.

"I don't trust him," Debbie said. "If there are other burial sites in here, he's bound to mess them up."

"Okay, let's follow them," Joe said. He looked for Dr. Beasley and Frank down by the riverbank. "You go ahead. I'll go let Frank and the professor know where we're going, and I'll catch up to you."

Taking advantage of the light from the flare, Frank and Beasley had headed upstream, skirting the edge of the bank, until they met the wall of the cavern. They were a few hundred yards ahead and Joe hurried after them.

"The only way to cross this river is to climb up above it, on that wall," Beasley was saying when Joe finally caught up to them.

Joe eyed the steep cliff skeptically. "It looks pretty smooth," he said. "Do you think there's anything to hang on to?"

Beasley went over to the wall, shined his light up it, then took off a glove and felt the damp rock. "There are plenty of handholds and toeholds," he said. "It wouldn't be too hard to get across." Removing his boots, he said, "I'll need one of you to hold an anchor rope."

"I'm heading over to the opposite side," Joe said in a quick whisper to Frank. "Spencer and Dirk went off in that direction. Debbie and I are going after them."

"Go ahead. I'll handle the anchor rope for Dr. Beasley," Frank said.

Suddenly they heard a shout from the far end of the cavern. In the dying light of the flare, they saw two tiny pinpricks of light heading toward them.

"Wait a second," Joe said. "There are only two lights."

"What do you mean?" Beasley said.

"Debbie went with them," Frank said. "There should be three."

"I don't like the looks of this," Beasley said. "Let's meet them halfway." He pulled his boots back on, and the threesome scrambled up the incline toward the skeleton wall, meeting Spencer and Dirk as they arrived, out of breath.

"Where's Debbie?" Frank said.

"There was an accident," Spencer said. "She fell. You have to help us."

"Fell? Where?" Frank said.

"Back there," Dirk said. He was panting heavily, and there was a long scratch across his cheekbone. "Down a sinkhole at the far end of the cave."

"So you just left her there?" Frank asked.

"We needed some rope," Spencer said. "Come on. We don't have any time to lose."

"It sounded like a bad fall," Dirk said. "We tried calling down to her, but we couldn't hear nothin' from her end. If she's alive, she could be in a bad way."

"Hey, Dirk," Joe said. "What happened to your face?"

Dirk wiped his hand against his cheek. "I guess I hit it on a rock."

"Must have been an awfully sharp rock to make a long scratch like that," Joe said.

"What're you getting at?" Dirk asked.

"Just that maybe something or somebody scratched you," Joe replied. "Like Debbie, just before you pushed her."

"What do you mean pushed her, you punk?" Dirk growled.

"Let me show you," Joe said, his temper rising. "You know, pushed her," he said, shoving Dirk in the chest. "Like that. Now do you get it?"

Dirk crouched down, charged, and threw a quick uppercut at Joe's jaw. Joe was ready, though. He sidestepped the punch to the left and connected with a right hook to Dirk's midsection. But what Joe didn't see was Spencer coming at him from the other side with a flying tackle.

Joe hit the dirt, shoulder first, with Spencer clinging to his back. The guy was little, but he was strong. Joe tucked and rolled hard to the left, kicking Spencer free and sending him crashing up against the skeleton wall.

Spencer grunted when he hit, landing in front of the wormhole and knocking loose a small avalanche of rocks and bones. Joe heard a huge grinding sound. He looked up and saw a slab of rock the size of a refrigerator coming straight at him.

Chapter

9

JOE EXECUTED TWO MORE quick rolls and dodged the giant block of stone by inches. But Spencer wasn't so lucky. The lower half of his body was pinned and he screamed in pain, his shout seeming to echo forever in the cave. With one hand he clawed at the dirt, struggling to pull himself free, and with the other he hurled skeleton bones and skulls every which way. "Get me out of here!" he yelled.

A skull rolled to rest at Joe's feet, its jaw yawning wide and its stained teeth grinning up at him.

"Just calm down and we'll work on getting you out," Frank said to Spencer. The boulder weighed at least a ton. Still, Frank put his shoulder against it and dug his hiking boots into the floor. "Come on, help me out," he shouted to the others. "Let's try to get some leverage on it."

Joe and Beasley were quick to join Frank. Dirk hung back until Beasley said, "Everybody. Let's go."

Spencer's face was twisted in pain, and in spite of the cool, damp air, he was starting to sweat. "Can you move it?" he said. "Just a few inches and I can scoot out. Come on, push."

The four of them gave it maximum effort, grunting and groaning for a full half minute, then they fell back exhausted.

"Forget it. We're never gong to move this thing," Joe said.

"If you two hadn't been fighting," Beasley said, "this would never have happened."

"If Dirk hadn't pushed Debbie—" Joe said.

"That's enough," Beasley said. "Let's just get Spencer out from under there."

"Hey, never mind him," Joe said. "What about Debbie? We don't even know if she's alive."

"I said enough," Beasley yelled. "We'll get to her in a minute."

Frank was shining his light around the base of the boulder where it had pinned Spencer's legs. He saw that the wormhole leading back to their base camp was completely blocked.

"Can you move your legs?" Frank asked.

"The left one, I can wiggle my toes. The right one not at all."

Frank knew that wasn't a good sign, but he didn't say anything. "Can I use your crowbar?" he asked Dirk.

"Be my guest," he said, pulling it out of his equipment bag. "But you ain't gonna have any luck against that boulder."

Frank jammed the crowbar under the stone and tried to pry it upward. Joe, Beasley, and Dirk each found handholds. On Frank's count, they all strained against the weight of the rock.

It started to tip up ever so slightly. "That's it," Spencer said. "It's moving. Keep it up." He started to inch himself out, first his hips, then his thighs.

All four of them were straining hard, pushing with all their might, but something under the rock slipped and it dropped back down. Spencer howled in pain again, arching his back and writhing against the dirt.

"Please. I can't take this," he said. "I can't take this anymore." He was panting under the stress, and Beasley did his best to calm him down.

"Just hang in there, Spencer," he said. "Let's get him wrapped up in a sleeping bag. We don't want him going into shock." He checked Spencer's pulse. "I don't think there's any major bleeding under there," he said. "His pulse is strong."

"Let's try lifting it again," Frank said.

"What's the point?" Dirk said. "That rock just settled down real nice. You're gonna need a backhoe to move it now. The thing we ought to be doing is cutting off the leg. Then we won't have to move anything."

"What?" Spencer said, gritting his teeth.

Frank grabbed Dirk's arm and said, "What are you trying to do, scare him to death?"

"I'm just telling it like it is," Dirk said.

Joe went over to Dirk and grabbed his shirt front. "That's enough out of you," he said. "You're taking me to where Debbie fell. And if it turns out you hurt her, I guarantee I'll hurt you."

"I didn't do nothin' to her, tough guy," Dirk said. "I came back here trying to get you to help me rescue her and you accused me of pushing her."

"Just show me where she is," Joe muttered, openly defying Beasley.

"All right, let's go," Dirk said. "Maybe these two geniuses can figure out how to move that rock while we're gone."

Joe gathered up some tools—a coil of rope, some steel anchor stakes, and an extra load-bearing belt—and said to Frank and Beasley, "We'll be back soon." Beasley didn't argue. He knew Joe was serious.

Dirk moved at a fast jog, almost as if he could

see in the dark. Meanwhile, Joe was struggling to keep up, stumbling every few yards. Within five minutes they reached the wall where Dirk had been inspecting the vein of coal.

"It's back in there," Dirk said. With the combined wattage of their helmet lights, Joe could make out a series of rooms carved into the limestone, almost like catacombs dug into the rock. "Which one?" he muttered.

"Near's I can recall she went back there in that one." He pointed to one of the openings in the rock wall.

"Show me," Joe said.

Dirk shined his light in Joe's face, and said, "Right this way, big guy." He turned and moved into the darkened room.

Joe followed, pausing beside Dirk to survey the room. Their lights swept across the floor, where Joe saw a series of holes—some the size of manhole covers, others the size of foxholes.

"Must'a been one of these," Dirk said.

Joe dropped the coiled rope beside his feet. "Come on," he said. "You know which one. You saw her go down."

With their lights trained forward, Joe heard Dirk reach into his equipment bag. He turned to see what he was retrieving, barely catching a glimpse of the shiny black automatic pistol before it was smashed against his ear.

Joe reeled, heard his helmet go skittering

across the rocks, and fell to the dirt, seeing stars. His ear was smarting from the blow and he was lying next to one of the holes, trying to get up.

"You want to see her so bad?" Dirk muttered. "I'll show you where she is. And you can stay down there with her. For good."

Joe felt Dirk's boot shove hard against the small of his back. He tried to get up, but Dirk shoved him again. "Hey," Joe yelled as he rolled over the edge and fell through space.

At the skeleton wall, Frank finished wrapping up Spencer. With sleeping bags covering his upper body, his temperature would be maintained, at least delaying the onset of shock.

Meanwhile, Beasley had done a thorough inspection of the rock, and he'd made an interesting discovery. "This stone looks like it was carved," he said. "Look at these corners. Limestone doesn't usually break in such neat lines."

"You think the Bone People had something to do with that?" Frank asked.

"Could be. Debbie might know," Beasley said. "Being a pre–Iron Age people, I doubt they had much in the way of tools, but look at this." He showed Frank a pair of grooves carved into the stone wall behind the boulder.

"It's almost as if somebody booby-trapped it," Frank said.

"It's probably some sort of gate," Beasley said. "It covers our wormhole just perfectly."

Frank felt a chill creep up his spine. "Maybe these skeletons are some kind of a warning."

"Maybe it's just a good old-fashioned trap," Beasley said. "And we're caught in it."

"There's always a way to unspring a trap," Frank said. "Let's look around."

Spencer, who had drifted into semiconsciousness, moaned and squirmed. "All right, Spencer," Beasley said. "I think we can figure this thing out."

Frank and the professor spent the next several minutes clearing more debris, and then they started searching the wall for clues. They discovered that the grooved tracks were slightly curved and the block of stone had two corresponding protrusions that fit into the tracks, while the corner worked on a pivot.

"If we can get that crowbar on this side," Frank said, "down near this pivot point, then we might be able to stand it back up in its original position."

"It's worth a try," Beasley said.

Frank grabbed the crowbar and was about to jam it under the rock when he heard Dirk's voice say, "Not so fast, kid."

Beasley and Frank swung their lamps around to find Dirk standing less than five feet away, aiming his automatic at them.

"Where's Joe?" Frank asked. "What did you—"

"Shut up," Dirk said. "And drop that crowbar."

"What are you doing with a gun down here?" Beasley asked sharply. "You fool."

"I'm the fool?" came Dirk's reply. "Or am I the genius? Seems like I just inherited a mother lode of coal, and I'm about to take care of the fools who are trying to stop me from mining it."

"What did you do to my brother?" Frank said.

"I said shut up and put down that crowbar, now!"

Frank raised the crowbar and let it fly, nailing Dirk's helmet and smashing his light before he knew what hit him. The gun went off with a loud roar and a flash in the dark.

Frank leaped away, heading down the slope toward the river.

He must have hit Dirk hard enough to knock the gun out of his hand because he didn't hear any more shots. He was scrambling fast, banging his shins on rocks, trying to navigate with the bobbing light on his helmet.

Frank tried to picture the cavern as he'd seen it the last time Beasley lit a flare. He figured the river crevice was directly in front of him. He veered off to the left, remembering where Dr. Beasley had tried to cross the river. It was his only escape route.

He moved quickly along the river's edge until

he found the wall. Where was Dirk? He glanced over his shoulder, but everything was black. Quickly he stripped off his boots, pocketed his gloves, and moved to the edge.

He reached out and felt for a hand grip, then a toe grip. He inched his way out over the river, clinging to the little pockets of stone.

Suddenly he heard Dirk's voice booming through the cavern. "I got you!"

Frank's stomach sank as a flare lit up the cave. Now he was an easy target.

"That's right, don't move," Dirk said. "This'll be real easy, just like shooting tin cans off a fence post."

Seconds later the first shot rang out. Frank's whole body jerked, but he kept his grip. The bullet smashed into the wall just above his head, raining fragments on him.

The second shot missed his left hand by inches, shattering his hold. His hand slipped, and he swung out from the wall.

He was clinging desperately by one hand and one foot when the last shot pulverized the stone up to his right, and he dropped straight into the rushing river.

The cold water took his breath away, soaking through his clothes and seizing him in its icy grip. He kicked to the surface, took a huge gulp of air, then was sucked down into a vicious whirlpool.

Chapter

10

TUMBLING THROUGH the ice-cold water, Frank felt a surge of panic. He was being pulled into a tunnel. What if there wasn't any place to come up for air?

The current was dragging him along fast and he knew it was pointless to fight it. He forced himself to relax and swim with it. Maybe he'd make it out of there faster.

Thirty seconds, forty. His heart was pounding hard, begging for oxygen. He reached up in the blackness and felt for the roof. There was no air pocket.

The pressure in his head was building and he knew he was about to pass out. Then he saw some glimmering lights. With his last ounce of strength, he swam hard for them, but they just seemed to get farther and farther away. Then everything went black.

The next thing Frank remembered, he was coughing hard and staring up into the face of a man who wore a baseball cap with the words Cathedral Cave State Park printed on it.

"Okay, folks, he looks like he's coming around," the ranger said. "Everybody, please keep your seats."

Frank couldn't stop coughing and spitting up water. Feeling as if he was going to vomit, he rolled over on his hands and knees.

"It's all right, kid," said the officer. "Let it all come up. You swallowed a lot of water."

Frank was starting to breathe at regular intervals, and he managed to choke out a few words. "Wh-where am I?"

A broad grin crept across the officer's face. "Why, you're in Cathedral Cave. Now I've got a question for you. Where'd you come from? And how'd you get in that water? You almost drowned."

"Other cave," Frank mumbled. Something was wrong with his mouth. His whole face was numb, and he couldn't work his tongue properly. He coughed again, turning on his side, then forced himself to sit up. He was starting to shiver uncontrollably. The officer wrapped his coat around Frank's shoulders.

"Other cave?" said the ranger. "What other cave?"

"Wh-where the s-skeletons are," he managed to say through chattering teeth. "Y-you've g-got to help us."

"Sure, I'll help you, son," the ranger said. "But first I've got to get you to the emergency medical unit. I radioed ahead for some assistance." He turned again to look over his shoulder. "I think he's just confused, folks. But he's going to be all right. Please, everyone sit down."

"No-no," Frank insisted. "I'm n-not confused."

He found himself looking at about fifteen tourists, all of them with cameras, all of them staring at him expectantly, as if they were waiting for Frank to make a speech. He was just as surprised as they were. They sat in two rows on benches that ran along the gunwales of a long, narrow boat. Frank was sitting in the bow. They were gliding through the calm waters of an underground lake.

Suddenly it hit Frank. Still shivering, he looked up at the arching cavern roof, where klieg lights had been fixed, illuminating the lake waters and the nearing shore. "I don't believe it," he said. "I just f-found the link."

"What's that you found, son?" the ranger said.

"I said the link to— Never mind. I'll explain when we get ashore."

As the boat pulled up to the dock, one of the

tourists took a picture of Frank, and the light from her flash blinded him for a second. He stumbled, then leaned heavily on the arm of the ranger, who led him to a waiting stretcher.

Two other park rangers helped carry Frank to a small clinic located next to the main cafeteria. Several of the tourists followed, but they backed off when the first ranger said, "He needs some rest, folks. He almost drowned out there, but the excitement's over now."

"My name's Frank Hardy," Frank said, untangling his hands from the coat wrapped around him and offering it to the ranger.

"Dan Mackleson," he said. "Pleased to meet you. Your hands are ice cold. Let's get you out of those wet clothes and into a blanket."

The ranger rummaged through a utility closet, pulled out some towels and blankets, and handed them to Frank.

"Thanks for saving my life," Frank said.

"We're all trained in CPR, and it's the least I could do," Mackleson replied. "You weren't even conscious when you surfaced. I was just giving my regular boat tour, when one of the tourists asked me what kind of fish they have in these underground lakes. I told her there weren't any, and she pointed over at you and said, 'Then what's that?' "

Frank grinned, wrapping the blanket around

his body and rubbing his hair with a towel. "You must have been surprised."

"Surprised? I've been doing this for nine years, and we've never had anything remotely like this happen," Mackleson said. "You still haven't said what you were doing out there, and where you came from."

Frank was starting to warm up—at least his shivering was under control. "I'm part of a caving expedition," he said. "We started over at Dismal Hollow, and we were trying to find a link to Cathedral Cave."

"Is that the same expedition Debbie Cameron's on?" Mackleson asked.

"You know Debbie?" Frank asked.

"Sure I do," replied the ranger. "I work with her."

"Well, she may be hurt," Frank said. "And my brother may be, too."

"What happened?"

"They fell—or were pushed—back in that other cavern. See, there's this guy, Dirk McCall—"

"McCall?" Mackleson said. "Is he the same McCall involved in the land dispute along the northern border of the park?"

"Right," Frank said. "He and his brother own the property now that his dad is dead. He went berserk. First he told us that Debbie had an accident. Then Spencer Lugo—he works for Dr.

Nick Beasley, the expedition leader—got caught under a boulder. When my brother, Joe, went with Dirk to see if Debbie was okay, Dirk came back alone and pulled a gun on us."

"He's got a gun?" Mackleson said.

"That's right, and he shot at me."

"Sounds like we've got a real emergency on our hands," Mackleson said.

"That's what I'm trying to tell you," Frank said. "And we'd better hurry."

"I'm calling out a red alert," Mackleson said. "I'll be right back."

One of the other rangers handed Frank a cup of hot soup and a spare state park uniform. Frank drank the soup and changed into the uniform. By the time Mackleson got back, he felt like his old self again—ready for action.

"We've got to go back up that underwater passageway," Frank said. "Do you have any diving equipment?"

"We've got a dive team on the way," Mackleson said. "They'll be here any minute."

"I'll go with them," Frank said. "I'm the only one who knows the way around on the other side."

"I know," Mackleson said. "But I don't want to be responsible for you getting hurt. We can't afford to be careless. There's a spring at the bottom of the lake, and the current is pretty strong."

"Don't I know it," Frank said. "It's more like a river. At least back in the skeleton chamber it is."

"Whatever it is, it's powerful," Mackleson said. "It comes into the bottom of Cathedral Lake about two hundred meters from the shore. Nobody's been very far into that tunnel, so we don't know much about it. How long would you say you were underwater?"

"Between a minute and a minute and a half," Frank said. "Say about a hundred ten seconds. I can't hold my breath any longer than that."

"We've tested the water in the tunnel and know it moves at about eight knots, and if it carried you for just a minute or two, then the chamber you came from can't be more than a couple hundred meters away," Mackleson said.

"You've got to give me some scuba gear," Frank said. "I've got my certification and plenty of experience."

Mackleson shook his head. "I told you. It's too risky. Cave diving isn't like regular scuba diving. I'm not letting you go back down there, and that's final." Frank scowled. "Just draw me a map and leave the diving to us," Mackleson said.

Twenty minutes later Frank sat alone in a boat anchored in the middle of the Cathedral Cave lake, watching the bubbles from the divers rise in the green-black water. The minutes ticked slowly by while Frank shined the beam of a searchlight down into the depths. All he could do was wait and try not to imagine the worst about what had happened to Joe and Debbie.

Joe came to at the bottom of a pit. His head was pounding, and his shoulder felt as if someone had dropped a safe on it. It was so black down there, he could hardly tell whether his eyes were open or closed. He tried to remember how he'd gotten there. Then it came back to him: first Dirk's sadistic grin as he pistol-whipped him, then his seeing stars and falling.

He tried to sit up, but the searing pain in his shoulder wouldn't let him. Regaining his composure, he tried it again, this time without putting any weight on the shoulder.

Joe strained to see, but it was too dark. He felt his face and his head, which was bare. Where was his helmet?

He patted the ground around him like a blind man who'd lost his cane. Dirt, pebbles, rock, but no helmet. He felt in his pocket for the book of waterproof matches, struck one, and squinted in the bright sulfury glare. Holding the match high, he searched around for his helmet.

What he saw instead was Debbie Cameron's body lying twisted on the ground less than ten feet away.

Chapter

11

JOE CUPPED HIS MATCH and went over to check Debbie's vital signs. He put his ear to her mouth and could sense she was breathing—but just barely. Then the match went out.

Joe felt for Debbie's helmet and carefully undid her chin strap. He turned the lever on Debbie's carbine light and hearing the telltale hiss of acetylene gas, lit another match and turned on the light. His shoulder was throbbing.

He looked up and saw a narrow chute like an empty elevator shaft that went straight up and out of sight. He was surrounded by hourglass-shaped columns of stone reaching from floor to ceiling. The chamber was dungeonlike, with a low ceiling and dank, stuffy air.

Keep calm. Keep your priorities straight, he told himself. First make sure Debbie is okay, then figure out a way to get out of here.

He touched Debbie's cheek. Her skin felt waxy and cold. Her breathing was shallow, her face was paste colored and bluish around the lips. He lifted one eyelid, and her pupil reacted to the light. That was a good sign. He hoped she was suffering only a mild case of shock.

Joe knew he would have to move fast. She was probably already developing hypothermia. He unfolded her emergency thermal blanket from inside her helmet and started to wrap her in it. It was made of thin sheets of plastic and reflective aluminum laminated together, specially designed to be extra light and insulating.

He lifted her head, and his hand came away moist with blood. Her hair was matted, and the ground underneath her head was soaked. She had a pressure wound on the back of her head, just under her hair line. She'd lost quite a bit of blood, which was probably why she was still unconscious.

Joe propped her up against one of the columns. Without any water or first-aid equipment, there wasn't anything else he could do but go for help.

He took a look around. The ceiling wasn't too high—about twelve feet. He figured the upper chamber wasn't more than fifteen or twenty feet beyond that. Any more than that and they would have been killed in the fall.

Should he yell for help? Frank would be looking for them, unless Dirk had shoved him down a hole, too. But if Joe yelled and Dirk heard him, Dirk would be back to finish the job. And he had the gun.

Joe examined one of the columns nearby, tracing its hourglass shape from floor to ceiling. He guessed that a stalactite growing down from the ceiling had met its companion stalagmite growing up from the floor. They had joined in the middle after centuries of infinitesimal growth, forming a single column from floor to ceiling.

He could see several of these formations by the light of Debbie's helmet lamp. He picked out the one closest to the chute in the roof. If he could get up inside there, he might just be able to make it.

All right, here goes, he said to himself. He grabbed onto the column and started climbing. The first half of the way was easy, but then it got tough. The hourglass shape forced him to lean backward as he clung to the column with arms and legs and shinnied up.

When he got close enough to the chute, he flung his right arm up and grabbed for a handhold on its inside wall. He tried to clamp on, but his hand came away and loose chunks of limestone clattered to the floor. He got a grip on the second try, and taking a deep breath, he swung out into space, hanging one-handed until he could grab the ledge with his other hand. Then he pulled his head and shoulders up into the chute, grimacing with the effort and the pain in his shoulder. He managed to get a leg up, then wedge himself into the chute and start inching his way up.

His shoulder was still throbbing, but he had to keep on climbing. It was their only hope. It was ten minutes before he hoisted himself into the chamber above.

The coil of rope lay where he'd dropped it. Good thing Dirk was in a hurry, Joe thought. He grabbed the rope and paused, listening carefully, but the place was silent as a tomb.

He decided to pull Debbie out rather than go for help. If she came to down there, she'd be helpless. He rigged a double-sling anchor rope around a nearby stalactite, then clipped on a load-bearing cam, cinching the loop. He dropped the rest of the coil down into the chute and it landed with a faint thump on the dirt floor below.

Threading the rope through the jammer on his webbed belt, he dropped back down the chute and made a soft landing at the bottom.

He found Debbie in the same position he had left her, but it looked as if the thermal blanket was helping. Her face wasn't so ghostly pale anymore, and her skin was warmer. As he was lifting her onto his back in a fireman's carry, he heard her groan.

"Debbie?" he said, setting her down again. "Can you hear me?"

She was definitely coming around. "What happened?" she said.

"You had a nasty fall," Joe said. "You cut your head, but you're going to be okay. I'm trying to get us out of here."

She touched the back of her head, wincing as she did so. "We had an argument," she said. "Spencer grabbed me, then Dirk hit me with his gun."

"Me, too. He seems to be doing a lot of that," Joe said.

"He said he didn't want anybody coming out of this cave alive," she said. "Except him and Lugo. They were analyzing coal samples when I came up behind them. I still can't believe Spencer brought an XRF gun down here."

"A what?" Joe said.

"An X-ray fluorescent spectrometer," Debbie replied. "It's a hand-held device used to measure the mineral content of whatever it's aimed it. It's a pretty specialized tool. Remember I was telling you we could have brought a tool with us instead of taking the burial site samples to the lab?"

"Oh, right," Joe said.

"Well, that's the gadget."

"And Lugo was using this ray gun to measure the coal?" Joe said.

"Most likely to gauge its purity," Debbie said.

"So he's the one prospecting for coal," Joe said. "I wonder if Beasley's in on the deal, too."

"It's an extremely pricey piece of equipment," she said. "I wonder where they got it."

"The university? The coal company?" Joe said. "Borrowed it? Stole it? Who knows?

"Hey," Joe continued. "I'm sorry about leaving you to follow those two on your own. That was stupid."

"Don't worry about it," Debbie said. "We should be worrying about your brother and Dr. Beasley. If Dirk jumped them, too, they could be in big trouble. He and Spencer are probably on their way to the surface right now, and they're not going to make it easy for us to follow."

"Actually, there was a cave-in," Joe said. "The wormhole leading back to base camp got blocked. Which makes them just as stuck as we are."

"What are you talking about?" she asked.

Joe explained how Spencer had been trapped by the boulder. "He's got at least one broken leg, maybe two," Joe said. "And that boulder is too heavy to move."

"So the burial site is ruined," Debbie said bitterly. "I just knew it. Once I get my hands on them, I'll—" She tried to stand up but stumbled, and Joe had to help her up.

"Why don't you just climb up on my back," Joe said. "I'll take us up. We'll do the fireman's carry." She nodded. Joe stooped and she climbed on his back, grabbing hold of him with both arms. "You okay?" he asked, standing up straight.

"Just go slowly," she said, "and we'll both be fine."

"Okay, hold on," Joe said, grabbing the rope with both hands and pulling their combined weight off the ground. They swung slowly back and forth while Joe anchored his feet against the rock pillar and tried to ignore the pain in his shoulder. Sliding the jammer up the rope and clamping it firmly, he pulled them to the top one notch at a time. It was a tight squeeze through the chute, but they made it up and out.

As he was coiling the rope at the top, Joe spotted his helmet at the back of the catacomblike room and went over to collect it.

"All right! It's still working," he said, lighting his lamp and fitting the helmet on his head. "Are you ready to roll?"

Debbie nodded.

"Just remember," he said. "The only advantage we have at this point is the element of surprise. Keep your light shielded. We don't want them to know we're coming."

Debbie paused for a moment. "You really seem to know what you're doing."

"Thanks," Joe said hastily. "I guess I'm just running on adrenaline."

"No," she said. "It's like you've been trained or something."

"It doesn't take any training to figure out that you can't shoot what you can't see. As long as we stay invisible we should be okay."

"I wish we had a weapon," Debbie said.

"If I remember correctly," Joe said, "didn't you say something about firearms being against the rules on an underground expedition?"

"The rules changed," Debbie said.

"What about that other gun, the one Spencer was using?" Joe asked. "Is it dangerous?"

"The XRF gun? Not like a conventional gun. It's got a tiny nuclear device in it. It shoots gamma rays, which are similar to X rays. Enough of them could destroy soft tissue."

As they approached the skeleton wall where Lugo was trapped, they kept their helmet lamps by their sides, pointed down at their feet, flashing them ahead only as far as they needed to mark a path.

When they got close to the wall, Joe could hear a low murmuring voice, like someone talking to himself. He motioned for Debbie to turn off her light, then he turned off his. They crept closer, and they could see Lugo lying all alone, wrapped in a sleeping bag, with a single candle burning in front of him.

Suddenly his murmuring stopped, and he glanced up. "Dirk? Is that you?"

Joe caught Debbie's arm, pulling her behind a rocky outcropping. Lugo's voice went a few notes higher. "Hey, who's that out there? Come on, Dirk. Stop playing games."

Suddenly Joe had an idea, and he whispered it into Debbie's ear. "See if you can spook him. Get him going, and maybe he'll flush Dirk out from wherever he's hiding."

She nodded. Taking a deep breath, she spoke in a raspy voice: "Why'd you let him do it, Spencer?" Echoing ominously in the darkness, her voice seemed to come from the back of the cavern.

Joe heard Spencer knock something over. A flashlight beam clicked on, piercing the blackness, searching the boulder-strewn cave for the source of the voice. "Who is that?" he said.

Joe and Debbie held perfectly still. Spencer's voice grew more hysterical. "Debbie?" he said. "Are you—"

"Why, Spencer? Why?" Again, Debbie's disembodied voice echoed all around the stone walls. It even sent a tingle up Joe's spine, and he had given her the thumbs-up signal.

"I didn't want to do it!" Spencer shouted. "It was Dirk's idea! He said it was the only way!"

His shouts echoed throughout the dark cavern, and his flashlight beam ricocheted wildly from side to side.

"I didn't do anything!" he wailed. "It wasn't me. I'm gonna die down here and rot like the rest of you. Oh, man, how did it end up like this?"

They waited for the echoes from Spencer's shouts to die down. For a few moments his terrified breathing was the only sound they heard until a shout came from down by the river.

"What's going on up there?" It was Dirk.

Joe whirled around, eyes searching the dark, until he saw the glimmer of two helmet lights down by the river crevice pointing in their direction.

"He took the bait," Joe whispered to Debbie. "Just let him come. I know I can handle him this time."

Chapter

12

JOE AND DEBBIE watched and waited in the dark as the two lanterns bobbed toward them. Joe wanted to time his attack perfectly. Soon the first light was close enough to make out Dr. Beasley's face. He walked stiffly past Joe's crouched form. Dirk followed close behind, his gun leveled at the middle of Beasley's back.

Joe waited until Dirk was almost past him, then stepped out from behind the rock and chopped him once hard on the wrist, knocking the gun out of his hand. Planting his left foot, Joe put every ounce of his weight behind a swift kick to Dirk's solar plexus.

The kick knocked the wind out of Dirk, and he crumpled, but Joe didn't let up. Before Dirk could straighten up, Joe knelt beside him, grabbed the bib of his overalls, pulled him up, and threw him on his back.

"Where's Frank, you scum?" Joe said. Dirk lay back for a second, then jerked his head up, temporarily blinding Joe with the beam from his lamp. The next thing Joe knew, a fist came crashing into his jaw, knocking him sideways, and Dirk squirmed free.

"Don't let him get away," Joe said, trying to clear his head. As his eyesight returned, he heard scuffling behind him.

"We got him," Debbie said.

"Let go of me," Dirk said.

Joe turned and his light revealed Debbie forcing Dirk's arm up behind his back and Dr. Beasley grabbing him by the front of his shirt.

"Thanks," Joe said, stepping over and grabbing Dirk's other arm. "Now let's find that gun."

Beasley let go of Dirk's shirt and swept his beam around the rocky floor. Within seconds, he said, "Right there," and went over to scoop up the automatic.

Joe grabbed a length of rope and quickly tied Dirk's wrists behind his back. Keeping a grip on Dirk's arm, Joe said, "Where's Frank?"

There was no answer.

"I said, *where's Frank?*" Joe said, giving Dirk's arms a sharp pull up behind him. Dirk let out a grunt but didn't answer.

"He shot him over by the river," Spencer said, his voice a weak monotone. "Two or three times. I heard it."

"You piece of garbage," Joe said. He wanted to strangle Dirk, but instead he grabbed both of his arms and wrenched them straight up behind him as hard as he could. "You killed my brother!"

Joe had no way of knowing that at that very moment, Frank was more than two thousand feet overhead, comfortably riding in the passenger seat of a truck driven by Dan Mackleson, Cathedral Cave State Park ranger.

Frank rolled down the window, and the warm air ruffled his hair. It was nearly nine o'clock, more than twelve hours since the expedition had first entered the cave at Dismal Hollow. He would have been enjoying this summer evening, but he was too busy thinking about his brother and the others, trapped underground.

The cave divers hadn't been able to swim up the tunnel leading from the Cathedral Cave lake to the skeleton chamber. The current was too strong. Their only choice was to drive overland to Dismal Hollow. While Ranger Mackleson was changing out of his wet suit, Frank had called Buddy to inform him about the accident.

"Sounds like you're gonna need some help," Buddy had said. "I'll get my equipment together. We'll go down there and see if we can straighten things out."

They had to take the same route the protestors had blocked when the Hardys were on the bus. The state police were letting vehicles through one at a time. There was enough light left in the sky for Frank to make out the protesters standing along the side of the road. He wondered how they'd react if they heard about what had happened on the expedition. With a coal mole flushed out, no telling what they might do.

"We're probably going to need some back-up," Frank said.

"I already called the state police and the county sheriff's office," Mackleson said. "They'll be meeting us up at the McCall place, along with an EMS team."

Ten minutes later they were climbing the steep dirt road in the gathering gloom. Their headlights finally picked out the McCall cabin as they turned into the driveway.

Buddy appeared on the porch wearing a pair of overalls and his caving belt. "I'm almost ready," he called down to Frank. "Just give me five."

"You can use my coveralls," Mackleson said to Frank. "And I've got some extra equipment in the back of the truck. It's not much—just a helmet, gloves, knee pads, a carbide light, and some rope."

"Thanks," Frank said, scrambling into the

back to grab the gear. He changed clothes under the porch next to the old truck that was on cinder blocks. He recalled it was Dirk's truck, left there when he sold its tires. It was a beat-up vehicle, dun colored, with shredded upholstery and plenty of rust in the body.

Frank heard Buddy slam the screen door, then he came down the stairs and stood beside the truck, adjusting his hat. "Ready?"

"Almost," Frank said, hooking the straps of his harness around his legs.

Buddy glared at Ranger Mackleson. Frank introduced him, but Buddy just nodded stiffly and said, "I don't need any outsiders to get involved in this. It's family business. I aim to take care of it myself."

"Sorry, but I can't let you do that," Mackleson said. "One of my colleagues is down there, and it sounds like she's in trouble. So it turns out it's my business, too."

"He's right, Buddy," Frank said. "You can't keep them out of this. We're talking about attempted murder here—maybe worse."

Buddy paused a moment, then shrugged. "All right" he said, "but do me a favor. Keep them police and sheriffs up here as long as possible. I don't want to have them down there messing things up."

"I'll wait up here for a while and do my best

to hold them off," Mackleson said. "Be careful—and good luck."

As they hiked through the dusk, their carbide lights showing the way, Frank noticed that Buddy was carrying a rusty old car jack on his tool belt. "What're you going to do with that?" he asked.

"You said Spencer Lugo got caught under a big boulder," Buddy said. "This is a ten-ton jack. Unless it's a twenty-ton rock, this should do the trick."

When they got to the campsite, the Gallagher twins had already turned in for the night. But they got up quickly, stoked the fire, and listened wide-eyed while Frank filled them in on the situation underground.

"We know Spencer's hurt," Frank said. "We're not sure what happened to Joe and Debbie, though."

"While you're down there, we'll set up an emergency treatment area down at the base camp," Alex said.

"Sounds good," Frank said. "When the EMS crew gets here, make sure you tell them we've got three possible casualties."

"You got it," Alex said.

Frank and Buddy went right into the cave. By now it was pitch black outdoors, so most of the bats were out on their nightly hunt for insects. But Frank could see a few hundred stragglers

118

still clinging to the ceiling, watching the two rescuers pass beneath them.

They slid down the rope Beasley had rigged to go after Joe and Spencer after the first cave-in. Frank led the way to the second rope, and they took the seven-hundred-fifty-foot drop to the base camp.

They found the camp undisturbed. The Gallaghers had delivered the rest of the supplies and set up a rudimentary camp kitchen. Frank's stomach rumbled at the thought of food, but it would just have to wait.

"The fishing line is anchored over here," he said, showing Buddy where Spencer had started marking their path. They followed the line as the trail wound around huge rocks and across black crevices.

Buddy moved quickly, as if he could see beyond the arc of his lantern. After Frank asked him to slow down for the third time, Buddy said, "Sorry, fella, but I practically grew up underground. Dirk did, too, until he got too uppity. My daddy always said he taught us to see in the dark. I feel like it worked for me. I don't know about Dirk."

Finally they reached the honeycombed wall where the expedition had crawled through the wormhole.

"Before this, you could feel the wind," Frank said, holding his hand in front of the narrow opening. "But not now that that boulder's blocking the other end."

"Wait a second," Buddy said. He moved along the wall and paused in front of each wormhole in turn. "Here it is," he said.

Frank joined him, kneeling to get his face closer to the hole, where he smelled that now-familiar earthy scent. "Do you think this one leads to the same chamber?" he asked.

"Can't tell," Buddy said. "But let's mark it, in case we can't unblock the other."

Buddy went in the other wormhole and Frank followed, keeping Buddy's feet in sight as they crawled. The first time, he hadn't felt claustrophobic. But this time, knowing the other end was blocked, he started to imagine there wasn't enough air to breathe. There sure wasn't much room to move. He kept banging his helmet on the roof or scraping his chin on the wet rock underneath him.

Frank found himself breathing too hard and sweating. All he could think of was getting out of this hole. He stopped, took a few deep breaths, and forced himself to concentrate on the task at hand. Then he started wriggling again, slowly but surely, and, after a few minutes, Buddy's feet stopped moving forward.

"Are we there?" Frank asked.

"I think so," came the muffled reply.

Frank heard metal clanking against stone.

Buddy must have been hammering. When he stopped, they heard Spencer's voice faintly saying, "Who's there? Who's making that noise?"

"It's us," Buddy said. "Me and Frank. Can you hear us?"

"Yeah" came Spencer's reply. Then, a second later, Frank could hear Joe's voice. "Frank? Is that you?"

"Sure is, Joe," Frank yelled, relieved to hear his brother's voice.

"We thought you were dead," Joe shouted. "Shot or drowned or something."

"No, I just went for a little swim," Frank shouted back.

"All right, y'all. I've got a car jack here," Buddy said. "I'm going to try to lever this boulder out from the wall."

"Okay" came the reply.

Frank listened carefully as Buddy forced the jack into position. Finally, he heard the ratchet gears working. "I think I got it," Buddy said. "Ready out there?"

"Ready," Spencer replied.

Along with the ratchet sound of the jack being cranked, Frank could hear a new sound with each thrust of the fulcrum—the grating of the huge block of stone being moved inch by inch.

Suddenly they heard Spencer scream, "Aahhh! Stop! Stop! It's crushing my leg!"

Chapter

13

AS SOON AS SPENCER SCREAMED, Buddy hit the release on the jack and the stone thumped back into place, sending a shudder through the rock under Frank's chest.

"It ain't gonna work from here," Buddy shouted through to the other side. "We're gonna have to try a different wormhole." He yanked the jack free with a clank. "Back up," he said to Frank. "No way we're getting through this way. Not without grinding Spencer's legs into hamburger. We gotta try the other hole, and fast."

Turning around was out of the question. The only thing to do was to back out, feet first. Frank thought crawling on his stomach was bad, but this was definitely worse. Now Buddy's boot heels were coming at him, and he really had to hustle so he wouldn't get kicked in the face.

"Easy does it, Buddy," Frank said. "I'm squirming as fast as I can."

"All right, pal, but we got to hurry," Buddy said.

Twenty minutes later Frank slid feet first from the wormhole. Buddy squirmed out and stood up, and Frank took a good look at him. He was scraped up and splattered with mud from head to toe. Frank realized he probably didn't look much better.

Frank turned toward the honeycombed wall and found the hole they'd flagged earlier. He checked for the cool, mossy cave wind. It was still there.

"I sure hope this one leads to the same cavern," Buddy said.

"Me, too," Frank said.

" 'Cause if it doesn't, we'll have to go back and jack that boulder free," Buddy said. "Never mind what it does to his leg."

"After you," Frank said, and stood back while Buddy climbed into the second hole.

Joe was so relieved to hear Frank's voice that he felt a little smug, even though they were still trapped on the other side of the boulder. "Three strikes and you're out, huh, Dirk?" he

123

said with a chuckle. "First Debbie, then me, then Frank. You're batting zero."

Dirk wouldn't look at Joe. He just stared at the ground. He was squatting on his heels, leaned up against a rock, with his hands tied behind him.

"Did you seriously think you'd get away with killing all of us?" Beasley asked. "Didn't you think somebody would notice when the entire expedition, except you, ended up missing?"

"Doesn't look like he's talking," Joe said. "Maybe you could answer that one, Spencer. Was that part of the plan? Once you found what you were looking for you'd arrange a few convenient accidents? Just wipe us out nicely and neatly, one by one?"

The graduate student glanced up at Joe. His face was pale and his eyes darted back and forth like those of a caged animal. "What am I supposed to know about it?" he said.

"I thought you two were partners," Joe said. "My brother and I saw you and Dirk talking together in the woods before the funeral."

"So?" Spencer said. "Is that a crime?"

"No," Debbie answered, "but helping shove me down that hole is. It's called attempted murder, and if you two are partners, I'll make sure you *both* get charged with it."

It was Spencer's turn to clam up.

Dirk, however, lifted his head upon hearing

Joe's news. "You saw him and me in the woods back behind the cabin?" he asked.

Joe nodded.

"That's good," Dirk said.

"What do you mean, good?" Spencer asked.

"Because that's when you told me about your plan to sabotage the expedition," Dirk said.

"That's a lie," Spencer said. "What're you trying—"

"He's workin' for Kentucky Coal and Shale," Dirk interrupted. "Just ask him."

"Is that true?" Debbie said.

Spencer refused to answer.

"If he won't talk," Joe said, "then I guess we'd better start looking for some physical evidence." He bent over the graduate student's knapsack to open it.

"Get out of there," Spencer said. "You don't have any right to search me."

"Just try to stop me," Joe said.

"What are you, some kind of cop?" Spencer asked.

"Keep quiet," Joe said.

Spencer tried to reach back and turn around to stop Joe from opening his pack, but he couldn't do it. He slumped back down and grimaced in pain.

"That's right. Just stay down," Joe said. "Don't try to fight it, because you'll just end up hurting yourself worse." Joe opened the pack, rummaged through it, and pulled out an electronic device.

"Let's see," Joe said. "What do we have here?"

It looked like a handheld TV remote control, only twice as large. It was heavy for its size, probably four pounds, and Joe thought maybe it had lead in it. It had a tiny LED screen on one end and a series of buttons on the other.

"That's it, the XRF gun," Debbie said.

"So, Spencer, how does this thing work?" Joe asked, taking aim at Lugo's head.

"Put that down," Spencer said. "It's dangerous."

"Let me see it," Dr. Beasley said. Joe handed it over, and the expedition leader took a close look. "The latest model—from Spectronics," he said. "Where'd you get this?"

Spencer didn't answer.

"Is it what Dirk just told us?" Joe said. "Did you get it from the local company?"

"I was going to donate it to the geology department," Spencer said.

"These things are worth a lot of money," Beasley said.

"What did they want for it, Spencer?" Joe said.

Lugo hesitated.

"Listen to me," Joe said. "If you want us to

126

pull you out from under that rock, you had better start answering some questions. Now."

"Don't forget," Debbie said. "Everything that happens down here, everything you do or say is going into my official report."

"You might want to give that some thought," Joe said to Lugo. "Especially when they charge you with attempted murder."

"They said I could keep it," Spencer said. He was mumbling, and they could barely hear him. "All—all they wanted to know was the carbon content of any coal we happened to come across. Just information. And I got to keep the gun. The geology department gets it."

Dr. Beasley activated the device, waited for its screen to light up, and then accessed its memory. It took a few seconds to call up the results of Lugo's test. "Looks like your analysis revealed some pure anthracite," he said, reading from the little screen. "A solid ninety-nine percent sample."

"That's right. That's my mother lode," Dirk piped up.

"And it stays right down here where it belongs," Debbie said.

"We'll see about that," Dirk muttered.

The second wormhole was narrower than the first, and Frank had to stop several times while Buddy forced himself through impossibly small spaces. Frank's elbows and knees were getting sore from the crawling, and his ears were ringing from banging his helmet on the roof.

"Hey, Buddy," Frank said, checking his watch. "It's been over half an hour. Do you think we're still headed in the right direction?"

"Can't tell, but we've got this far so we might as well go all the way to the end," came Buddy's muffled reply.

They crawled for another ten minutes in silence. Finally Frank heard Buddy say, "Looks like we found something." His feet disappeared as he dragged himself out of the tunnel. Frank followed him and once he was clear he bounced to his feet. They were in a big chamber, and Frank was dizzy with the sense of space. "Hey," he yelled. "Anybody out there?"

"Is that you, Frank?" came Joe's voice, echoing through the chamber. Frank looked back to his left and made out several lamps illuminating the base of the skeleton wall.

"All right," Buddy said, clapping Frank on the back. "We did it."

"It's us, Joe," Frank said. "Over here."

Frank and Buddy headed toward the lights, and they could hear somebody scrambling toward them. Within a couple of minutes, Joe came into view, hurrying to meet them halfway.

"What took you guys so long?" Joe asked.

"Sorry. We had to take the long way round," Frank said.

"At least you made it in one piece," Joe said. He led them back to the boulder.

Buddy took one look at his brother and said, "You're a worse fool than I thought." Dirk didn't answer.

Next Buddy turned to Lugo. "Sit tight. We're gonna get you out of there now." He unstrapped the car jack from his tool belt, and he and Frank started to inspect the boulder. Frank showed him where and how it had fallen.

Meanwhile, keeping an eye on Dirk, Joe noticed that Dr. Beasley had taken Debbie aside. He was handing the XRF gun to her.

"You could use this to check the age of these skeletons," he said.

"That's a great idea," Debbie said. "Using the coal company's little machine against it."

"What do you mean?" Joe asked.

"Well, we can analyze the chemical content of the bones just as they analyzed the content of the coal," Debbie said. "That way we can estimate the age of the bones. It'll help prove this site is prehistoric."

"Just make sure you don't zap those skeletons too hard," Joe said. "I think I've already demonstrated how fragile they are."

"It's all right," Beasley said. "The gun's got a beam modulator, kind of like a volume control.

Besides, it doesn't create any vibrations that I know of."

"Okay," Buddy said, "we're gonna need some help over here in a second."

Debbie handed the XRF gun back to Dr. Beasley and said, "You seem to know how the thing works, Nick. Why don't you zap them?"

"Right," he said, and started to punch instructions into the device's keyboard.

Joe and Debbie went over to help Buddy and Frank, who had wedged the jack into a niche between the cave floor and the boulder. Buddy used the ratchet lever to bring the lifter arm in contact with the stone. Now he needed some help from Joe to start pumping the handle up and down. Meanwhile, Frank took hold of Spencer's shoulders, ready to start pulling. He had his lamp trained on the spot where Lugo's legs were pinned.

"It's moving," Spencer said. "I can feel it. Please don't let it fall on me again."

Buddy and Joe grunted with the effort of cranking the jack. The stone rose an inch and then another.

"Grab my hands," Frank said to Spencer. Grimacing, Spencer latched onto both of Frank's forearms as Frank leaned back and pulled. The jack ticked up a couple more notches, and Frank dragged Spencer free.

"Watch it, fellas!" Buddy yelled. Just as Spencer's feet cleared the boulder, it tipped to the right and rolled away from the wall, crushing several more skeletons under its weight.

The boulder kicked up a cloud of dust that filled Frank's lantern light. He heard somebody coughing.

"You're clear," he told Spencer, letting go of his arms.

Spencer just lay there, breathing slowly, rigid with pain. Buddy crouched beside him, fanning some dust out of his face. "Let's see here," he said. He whipped out his pocketknife and slit Spencer's pant leg from ankle to hip.

Spencer's leg reminded Frank of something he'd seen once after a motorcycle accident. It was swollen to almost twice its normal size, with a nasty-looking scrape at the knee. The foot was wrenched into an unnatural position, with the toes pointing inward at almost a right angle.

"Debbie," Buddy said, "do you think you could take a look at this? After the nice job you done on my arm, I reckon you got a knack for patchin' folks up."

Debbie glared at Dirk, then at Spencer. "Your brother and this one tried to kill me," she said. "I feel like—"

"So do we, Ranger," Frank said. "But if we can get them to the surface without killing them, they're going to be hit with some very serious charges. The sheriffs and the state police are already up there. I'm sure they're itching to take our statements."

"Debbie, please—I'm really sorry," Spencer said. "I swear I'll make it up to you. I'll testify. I'll do anything you want me to. Just get me out of here alive."

"All right. Stop babbling and just hold still," she said, tracing her fingers down the shin bone from the knee to the ankle. A few inches above the ankle she paused. "I'd say the break is here. Or at least the main one. We're going to need a splint."

"How about a couple of struts from one of the backpacks?" Frank said.

"Buddy, can you handle that?" Debbie said.

"Yes, ma'am," Buddy said. "No problem." He grabbed one of the backpacks and using the tools from his belt, started to dismantle it. A few minutes later he held two aluminum struts, each about a foot and a half long.

"Okay," Debbie said. "These should be stiff enough." She placed a strut on either side of Spencer's shin bone. "We'll use plenty of tape top and bottom to stabilize the fracture," she said. "But I'm going to have to set the bone first."

"No," Spencer said. "Please."

"We have to," Debbie said. "You know exactly what could happen. A loose bone fragment gets in a vein, goes to the heart and, bingo, no more Spencer to testify at the trial. Okay?"

"Okay."

Frank pulled the first-aid kit out of his pack and handed it to Debbie. He also pulled out a towel for Spencer. "Bite into that," he said. "So you don't have to scream."

It didn't take long to set the leg, but Frank had to hold Spencer's arms down to keep him from thrashing around. Lugo bit down hard on the towel while Debbie gave his foot a quick twist, pulling down on the leg at the same time. Then she taped the aluminum bars to either side.

"That ought to suit you well enough for travel," she said, "but don't try to walk on it."

"Thanks," Spencer managed to say.

"All right," Frank said. "Let's rig up a sleeping bag as a stretcher and get out of here."

"It's about time," Joe said. "I feel as if we've been down here for two weeks."

Dr. Beasley had finished taking the readings of the bones, and he was peering at the XRF gun's small LED screen. "It's official, folks," he said. "The hydration rims measure five microns."

"We're talking tens of thousands of years old," Debbie said.

Dr. Beasley went over to his knapsack near where Dirk was crouched. He switched the XRF gun off and was about to put it in his pack when Dirk sprang from his crouch, grabbed the gun in one hand and caught Beasley in a choke hold with the other. He held the XRF gun against the professor's temple, pointing it straight into his eye.

"Anybody makes a move and I burn his eye out," Dirk growled.

Chapter

14

EVERYONE STOPPED.

"How did you—" Joe said.

"Shut up, punk," Dirk yelled. "Did I tell you to talk?"

"Stay calm, Dirk," Frank said. "Just take it easy. Nobody's going to do anything."

Dr. Beasley started to struggle, trying to grab hold of Dirk's arm and loosen the choke hold. But Dirk just choked him harder and with a vicious twist of his arm brought the professor to his knees, pressing the XRF gun harder against his temple.

"If you don't quiet down, Doc, I'm gonna fry your brain," Dirk said. "I swear I'll do it."

Beasley froze and Dirk released the choke

hold, then patted down the professor's coveralls with his free hand. It didn't take him long to find his automatic pistol in Beasley's back pocket.

Meanwhile Joe was still trying to figure out how Dirk had gotten loose. Looking at where Dirk had been squatting down, he noticed a few shredded strands of rope clinging to a sharp edge on the rock. Joe realized that he must have been working it slowly the whole time.

Dirk clicked off the safety and checked the ammo clip on the automatic. Then he tossed aside the XRF gun and waved the muzzle of his pistol at the group.

"I want y'all where I can see you," he said. "Get on over there close to Spencer, you hear?"

Frank was just hoping everybody would stay cool. The thing to do was to lull Dirk into thinking they were easy prisoners, then watch him closely and when he got distracted, make a move.

"Come on, Ranger," Dirk said to Debbie, who was slow to join the others. "Let's move it." He pointed the automatic at her head. "I know you're probably lined up with them anticoal protestors that were blocking the roads and such."

"Actually, I'm not with—"

"Shut up!" Dirk said. "Or else you're gonna wind up like that other one.

"Now, was that you, professor, who was telling me about who could or could not do such and such with my land?" Dirk continued.

"That was me," Debbie said. "And I wasn't saying—"

"That's right," Dirk said. "You wasn't saying anything. And you still ain't. So shut your mouth!"

"Leave her be," Buddy said, stepping forward. "You got no reason to be messing with these here strangers, Dirk. If you want to get rough with someone, you can take me on, just like you always tried to."

Dirk's laughter filled the cavern. "See those bones, brother?" He gestured at the skeletons that still looked down from the wall, propped up like a silent audience to Dirk's antics. "How'd you like to join them up there?"

"Just you try it," Buddy snarled.

"Take a look around, everybody," Dirk said, waving the gun to include the entire group. "Get used to your surroundings, because it'll be a long time before anybody finds out about you, and when they do I'll be long gone."

"I'm with you, Dirk," Spencer said.

"Forget it, Spence," Dirk said. "You're not any good to me with a broken leg. You expect me to drag you all the way back to the surface, just so you can play the middleman between me and whoever wants to buy my coal? I ain't that stupid."

"But we made a deal," Spencer said.

"Deal's off," Dirk said. "I can negotiate with them just as well as you can. I don't need you no more."

"You're right," Frank said. He wanted to keep Dirk talking, get him to let down his guard for a second. "You don't need any of us anymore. You can do what you want. But what are you going to do about all the cops waiting for us up there?"

Dirk hesitated. Then he said, "There's lots of ways out of these caves. I reckon I can dodge the police, one way or another."

"And then what?" Frank said. "There's too many loose ends. You've got nowhere to go. You can hide for only so long. And besides, what good will that do you?" As he talked, Frank took a slow step to the side, away from the group. "If you just hand over the gun now, they'll take that into account when they charge you. At least you won't go up for murder, because nobody's dead. And if you go quietly, they'll probably even consider a plea bargain. You've already lost any chance of selling your land. It's over, Dirk. You might as well give up now."

Frank was taking another careful step sideways when Buddy's helmet came flying out of nowhere. Then Buddy charged in behind it and jumped Dirk.

Dirk dodged the flying helmet and squeezed off a shot, but he was already going down under his big brother's crushing weight. Frank heard the bullet ricochet off the wall behind him, and he leaped on top of the wrestling brothers, going for the gun. Frank grabbed a wrist. He couldn't tell whose finger was on the trigger, but the gun went off with a loud bang.

The flash burned Frank's hand, and the report deafened him. He heard Dirk grunt and he rolled away, cradling his fingers. When he looked up, he saw Joe struggling with Dirk. Joe tried to wrench the gun from Dirk's grip, but Dirk twisted free, and holding his side, loped off toward the river, disappearing into the darkness.

Frank was on his feet, trying to focus his light on Dirk's retreating form. He thought he saw him duck down behind a boulder, but when he got there Dirk was gone. Joe was right on his heels, followed by Buddy.

"Did you see where he went?" Joe asked.

Frank shrugged. "Can't tell."

"You two stay put here with the others," Buddy said. "Let me finish this once and for all."

"No way you're going after him alone," Frank said. "I don't like the way you McCalls settle your differences."

"Let's fan out," Joe suggested.

"He doesn't have a light," Frank said, "and he's shot. He won't go far."

"Do we have any more flares?" Joe called out.

"No," Beasley said. "We're out. Do you want some help down there?"

"That's okay," Frank said. "You stay with Debbie and Spencer. We'll be right back."

The Hardys and Buddy spread out, each one searching behind boulders and into crevices. Frank found a bloody hand print on a rock near the bank of the river. He called Joe and Buddy over, and they soon found a footprint.

"He's heading upriver," Joe said. "Let's go get him."

The trail led all the way up to the cavern wall. Every few yards there was a telltale shoe print or drop of blood. Frank was the first to train his lamp out over the river, where he framed Dirk, clinging to the rocky cliff, attempting to cross the river.

"Back off," Dirk said. "I still got my gun."

"Come on, Dirk, it's over," Frank said. "You're hurt. Come back to this side. We'll bandage up that wound."

Dirk's eyes looked glassy as he glanced back at their lights.

"Then what?" he shouted, waving the automatic at them. "What do you got planned for me then? Fix me up a nice little square room in the state pen, with bars on the windows and an hour a day in the exercise yard? You gotta be out of your mind."

"C'mon, Dirk," Buddy said. "Nobody's gonna take you to no state penitentiary. Ain't nothing gonna happen to you if you just come on back with us."

Dirk didn't respond.

"Come on, Dirk," Buddy said. "We can help you out of this."

"You know that's a bald-faced lie," Dirk said, a deadly calm coming into his voice. "I'm warning you for your own good. If any of y'all come after me, I promise I will take you with me."

With that, he let go of the wall, fell into the black water, and was gone in a flash.

Joe's first impulse was to dive in after him, but Frank caught his arm. "Too risky," he said. "I'll go get a rope."

Joe stood on the edge of the river and shined his lamp down into the water, searching back and forth.

"I don't see him, do you?" Joe asked. Buddy was searching the swift black water with his carbide lantern, too. He shook his head.

At least twenty seconds passed in silence, then Joe spotted Dirk's head breaking the surface farther downstream. He heard him gasp loudly for breath.

"There he is," Joe shouted. Almost out of reach of their lights, Dirk's face showed up pale against the inky water surrounding it. A leering grin as he was pulled quickly downstream was the last they saw of him before he disappeared into the whirlpool.

Chapter

15

FRANK CAME BACK with a coil of rope and found Joe and Buddy staring at the place where Dirk's face had disappeared underwater.

"We saw him right over there," Joe said, pointing.

"He might make it," Frank said. "It took me a minute and a half to two minutes to wind up in Cathedral Cave."

"If he can hold his breath that long," Joe said.

"Sure," Buddy said. "Only problem is, he can't swim."

"That definitely could be a problem," Joe said. "He seems like one of those guys with nine lives, though. I wouldn't be surprised if we hear from him again."

They turned to hike back up to the skeleton wall. When they got to the wormhole, Frank told the others about Dirk's latest escape.

"If he ends up in the Cathedral Cave lake," Debbie said, "shouldn't we try to hustle our way up to the surface? Maybe the rangers could intercept him somehow."

"If he didn't drown then he's already there," Frank said. "Either somebody grabs him or he's long gone. It's too late for us to catch him. Unless somebody feels like holding his or her breath for about three minutes and going for a very dangerous swim."

Nobody did. Instead, they decided it was time to break camp and head back up to the surface. Frank helped Debbie and Buddy put Spencer into the sleeping bag. Buddy volunteered to drag him through the passageway.

Before leaving the cavern, Debbie took one last look at the skeletons—the ones that were still propped up on the wall and the ones that had been crushed by the boulder. With a sigh and a shake of her head, she said, "At least we got some photos and a good look at them before the whole place got trashed. That way we can reconstruct it later."

"Maybe you should just leave it the way it is," Joe said. "After all, the Bone People's trap worked. Isn't that the way they would have wanted it after someone came barging in here?"

"You've got a good point, Joe," she said, "but we'll leave it to someone higher up than I am to decide."

With Debbie and Beasley leading, Buddy dragged Lugo behind him through the winding tunnel. Frank and Joe took up the rear. They could hear the grad student moan and complain every once in a while when they hit a bump or had to squeeze around a bend.

When they got to the larger chamber, Frank volunteered to go up to the base camp with Dr. Beasley for the stretcher. Buddy, Debbie, and Joe propped Spencer up against the wall of the cavern. He promptly fell asleep and they waited.

After a long silence, Debbie spoke to Joe. "I mentioned this before, but you and your brother seem almost like professionals. Tell me the truth—are you two undercover cops?"

Joe raised his eyebrows. "What makes you say that?"

"You know exactly what I'm talking about. The way you've been handling yourselves since you got here. I've seen a lot of student assistants on a lot of caving expeditions, and you two are different. Better trained, more poised, more mature."

"You're getting warm," Joe said. "And if you keep throwing us compliments like that, I might just tell you everything."

"So tell," she said.

"I can't right now. I can promise some information, though, if you give me some first."

"I'm going to hold you to your word," Debbie said.

"My word is good," Joe said.

"So what do you want to know?" she said.

"For starters, who set that fire under Beasley's tent?"

She gave him a level stare. "Oh, come on. You're not going to accuse me of that again, are you?"

"If it wasn't you, it had to be Spencer," Joe said. "But why bother? This whole case makes sense except for a couple of loose ends like that."

"Case?" Debbie said. "You *are* a cop, aren't you? Exactly who are you working for?"

"Our dad," Joe said. "He's a private investigator. Frank and I help him out sometimes. He has a very important client who had an interest in what was going on with this expedition. That's all I can say right now, at least until I get clearance."

"As long as you're not working for the coal company," she said.

"We're not," Joe said.

"From the minute I saw the way you handled Buddy's rifle," she said, "I knew there was something suspicious about you."

"The feeling's mutual," Joe said. "Except

maybe I thought you were acting *un*profes-sional. You just seemed awfully opinionated for a park ranger. You had that run-in with Beasley, and the next thing we knew his tent was on fire."

"Spencer set me up," Debbie said. "It's obvi-ous. He smeared the ashes on my tent."

"I understand that, but why would he want to get rid of Dr. Beasley?" Joe wondered.

Just then Spencer woke up with a groan, and Buddy bent down to take a look at him.

"He don't seem too good," Buddy said.

"Let's see," Joe said. He went over and un-zipped Spencer's sleeping bag. His face was pale, and his eyes were half closed. Debbie checked out the broken leg.

"Hey, Spencer, can you hear me?" Joe said.

Spencer opened his eyes wide and said, "Yeah." His voice was hoarse.

"Frank will be back with a stretcher pretty soon," Debbie said. "You should be all right once they get you to a hospital."

"Thanks for helping me," he said. He paused, looking up at the three of them. "I guess this is all my fault," he said. "I thought I could earn some quick money and get into the coal pros-pecting business. I thought it would be simple."

"That doesn't explain why you set Dr. Beas-ley's tent on fire," Joe said.

"He was starting to suspect me," Spencer

said. "Remember, he's been in my position. He did some prospecting himself when he was my age. There isn't a lot of money pouring in when you're still a student at the age of twenty-six. A person's got to earn a living."

"So you decided to torch Beasley and blame it on me?" Debbie asked.

"I didn't really need either of you, once the expedition got going," Spencer replied. "That's why I splattered the battery acid on the rope. Maybe if there was an accident and one or both of you were out of the picture . . ."

"You could concentrate on looking for coal instead of the link to Cathedral Cave," Debbie said.

"That's right," Spencer said. "Dirk and I got to talking. He told me about that restrictive covenant. I guess his dad was about to sign it. I figured Dirk and I could be partners."

"You'd help him find the coal under his land," Joe said, "and he could cut you in on the eventual deal with the coal company. All you needed was a little carefully planned sabotage to stop the expedition from finding the link to Cathedral Cave."

"Then we stumbled on those skeletons," Spencer said. "We pushed Debbie down the hole, then I got trapped and Dirk just went out of control."

"That was when your whole plan unraveled," Joe said.

Just then Frank and Dr. Beasley returned with the stretcher—a board with straps to hold the victim and handles all around for easy transport.

"The Gallaghers are standing by," Frank said. "The state cops rigged up an electric winch. The trip back up is going to be a breeze this time— just like riding an elevator."

"That's a relief," Joe said. "I think I've had enough of rope climbing."

With Buddy, Frank, Joe, and Debbie each on a corner, they carried Spencer on his stretcher, making their way slowly over the rubble-strewn cave floor.

Within an hour, just as the sun was rising over the cliffs of the hollow, they came out. The emergency team met them on the ledge outside the cave mouth and carried Spencer down to the trail then back up to the McCall cabin where the ambulance was parked. They would have a hefty police escort on the way to the hospital.

Frank spotted Ranger Mackleson sitting on a boulder by the edge of the stream, talking to the Gallagher twins. The ranger stood and waved as Frank approached.

"This is my brother, Joe," Frank said, "and you know Debbie Cameron."

"I sure do," he said. "Nice work down there, Debbie."

"Thanks for all your help up top, Dan," she said.

"Just doin' my job, ma'am," he replied.

"Did you contact park headquarters, Dan?" she asked. "Because there's reason to believe that Dirk McCall is—"

"They found him," Mackleson said. "I heard it on the radio about an hour ago. He floated up in the Cathedral Cave lake. He was drowned."

Everybody looked at Buddy, but nobody said a word. The news of his brother's death didn't seem to shock him much. He just looked down at his boots for a while.

"Well, I'll have to get used to this, I guess," he finally said. "Bad people, they often do come to a bad end. Dirk and I weren't close since he went to jail that first time. He was a nasty, scrappy fella, always in trouble, but he was my brother. With him gone, plus Pop, that leaves me alone. I'm the last McCall in these parts."

"You've got your father's land," Frank said.

"That's true," he said. Looking at Debbie he said, "And we could take up that restrictive covenant idea again. Only this time, we could make it stick."

"That would be great," Debbie said. "I think we can pretty much count on the state park backing you financially. Maybe they can figure out a way to pay for your back taxes and your mortgage. You could probably lease the property to preserve it for caving research and for an extension of the state park to include the new ancient burial sites."

"Do you think there's a job in it for him?" Frank asked.

"I don't see why not," Debbie said. "We could always use a ranger who knows the caves backward and forward."

"And who can see in the dark," Joe added.

"Y'all got uniforms in my size?" Buddy asked.

"That should be part of the deal," Joe said. "Custom-made park ranger outfits."

"Thanks, Joe," Buddy said. "But seriously, Deb, you think I could qualify as a park ranger?"

"We don't discriminate," she said. "We've got all types. You name it."

"Well, then, sign me up," Buddy said.

As they all headed back toward the McCall cabin to make their statements to the police, Dr. Beasley thanked them for their efforts and promised they would all be made honorary members of the university geology department.

"But more importantly," the professor said, "what are we going to name the link?"

"It's traditional to name new passageways after their discoverers," Debbie said.

"How about Beasley's Tunnel?" Frank said. "It's got a nice ring to it, and it was Dr. Beasley's expedition."

"Forget it, Frank," Beasley said. "You found it, and it almost drowned you. So Frank's Link it shall be."

"Frank's Link?" Frank said, looking a little embarrassed.

"I don't know," Joe said. "It sounds like some new kind of hot dog to me."

"Would you settle for Hardy Passage?" Beasley said.

"That sounds a whole lot better," Joe said. "Now let's go call Dad and give him the good news. We've got an underground tunnel named after us. Yee-haw!"

Frank and Joe's next case:

Frank and Joe have come halfway around the world to investigate sabotage on a movie set. India's culture and customs may be foreign to them, but when it comes to battling terror, neither brother is a stranger to danger. And as soon as they set foot in this land of mystery, it's bombs away over Bombay! The Hardys rush to the movie set, where there are lights, cameras, and nonstop action. Someone's determined to put them out of commission by whatever means necessary: powerful explosives, razor-edged machetes, a cobra's poisonous fangs. The Hardys can't afford to miss their mark . . . because this is one flick sure to have a killer climax . . . in *Acting Up*, Case #116 in The Hardy Boys Casefiles™.